RENEGADE

RENEGADE

DAMIAN'S CHRONICLES™ BOOK TWO

MICHAEL TODD   MICHAEL ANDERLE
LAURIE STARKEY

PROLOGUE

FOURTEEN YEARS PRIOR

Chris yelled a challenge as he danced tauntingly across the room. "Let's see if you motherfuckers can keep up with Chris's magical dance steps."

He crossed his feet and spun, keeping his arms outstretched, and shot the demons around him. Korbin ducked as a bullet flashed past him and struck the wall. "Hey, Dance Fever, can you chill out a little? I want to get back without bullet holes."

"Oh, yeah. Sorry, man. My bad." He aimed quickly, pulled the trigger, and shot a demon in the face.

Damian chuckled and looked back down at the demon he held. He closed his eyes and began to exorcise it. "*Sancti Michaelis Archangeli Illustris princeps caelestis exercitus, defende nos in proelio adversus principes et potestates, adversus mundi rectores mundi tenebrarum et spiritus meus in excelsis. Custodem et patronum sancta veneratur Ecclesia eius, quam vobis. Dominus præcepit tibi negotium ut de ducens in animis*

1

hominum redemptorum beatitudine caelesti. Orate Dominum ut projicerent de pace nostra pedibus et Satanas, et adhuc ab eo ut servare tenens fecerit homo, et captivi ducentur in Ecclesiae nocere. Benedictus Deus ad throni misericordiae Domini esse potest venire cito tenendam et pecus antiquus serpens Satanas et daemonia mittentes eum in catenis in abyssum, ut non seducat amplius gentes."

The creature thrashed frantically before it exited and left the woman's body lying quietly and normally on the floor. Screeches echoed from the light as it rose above her and hovered in the air. Finally, it burst and showered everything in its radius with ash. One of the other team members, Charlie, squinted at Damian. "Hey, uh, priest? You think if you're gonna save these wretched souls, you could keep your demon corpse dust over there? I'm breathin' this shit into my lungs here."

He raised his hand and nodded. "Sorry, sorry. That was a feisty one."

The other man pointed behind the priest. "That one looks feisty too, bro."

He swung, raised his pistol, and pulled the trigger. The bullet struck the creature between the eyes, and it immediately turned to dust. Damian felt like he had broken his oath every time he killed a demon without attempting an exorcism, but there were too many of them. He'd made a promise to the church, though, and he would do whatever he could to exorcise before killing.

Three demons ran to the side, and Damian headed after them. He increased his speed, his breath labored. A pile of rubble at the side of the old dilapidated warehouse provided a handy ramp and he leapt off it with his arms extended. He grabbed one of the creatures by the feet, and they tumbled across the ground until he managed to scramble on top of it. He held out his cross, this time going for the shorter version of the exorcism. "*In nomine Domini omini ego mittam te, daemonium. Quo pertinent ad inferos. In nomine Patris et Filii et Spiritus Sancti. Amen.*"

The demon rose from the man and clawed at its throat and limbs as it screamed at the top of its lungs. Damian turned his head and closed his eyes as it exploded, then scrambled to his feet and lunged toward the other two, who had stopped to watch. He grabbed one and slugged it hard across the cheek, knocking it to the ground. Holding it down with his weight, he began the exorcism, but the third swiped relentlessly at him. Knowing he had no choice, he lifted his pistol and shot the attacker in the head, made the sign of the cross over his chest as it fell, and its body turned back into human form.

He looked down at the demon beneath him, angrier than hell. "If you fuckers would only hold still, I could work, and no one would have to die!"

Once he'd successfully exorcised the demon, he stood and wiped his hands on his legs. Chris joined him and looked down at the human, who was alive but unconscious. "You did good work there, buddy."

Damian wiped the sweat from his forehead. "Yeah, but getting them to that point by myself is hell."

His companion slipped his pistol back into its holster and shrugged. "I've had your back this far. Not gonna stop now. I'll bag 'em, and you give them that Jesus juice?"

The priest chuckled as he nodded. "Hell, yes. Let's do this."

Together, they raced through the warehouse. His teammate subdued the creatures, and he exorcised them as quickly as he could. As another demon left a body, Chris approached, holding out both hands. Two infected dangled in the air, each trapped in a large fist, and they squirmed to free themselves. "How about these two fuckers?"

Damian stood and held his cross out as he recited the exorcism prayer. To his surprise, it worked on both at the same time. As the creatures released the bodies, Chris lowered the unconscious forms to the ground. He looked at Damian with an impressed nod. The priest flipped his cross in his hands. "Never done *that* shit before."

His teammate laughed and slammed his elbow into a demon's face without looking. "First time for everything. Very convenient, and saves time, too."

He chuckled as he followed the man and bent to exorcise each unconscious Damned they encountered. It was like an assembly line, he thought irreverently. Chris knocked them out, and he saved their souls. As he repeated the exorcism over another body, his partner cleared his throat. "Uh, a little help here?"

He looked up to see the fighter with his back against the wall. Four demons snarled and slashed at him. Damian straightened and hurried forward, leapt through the air, and landed on one of the creatures' backs. He drew his gun, and shot twice to the right and once to the left. *Three down, one to go.* The fourth twisted and fought, trying to throw him off.

Chris stepped forward and pushed up his sleeve. "Arms up, D."

The priest held on with his legs and put his hands in the air. His partner reared back and struck the demon in the face as hard as he could. Damian jumped off, and the creature hit the ground. He stood over it and tilted his head to the side. The demon had partially taken over the woman it possessed. She now had the body of a woman and the head of a demon and wore red lipstick.

Chris put his hand on his chin and shook his head. "Now we have drag queen demons?"

Damian pursed his lips. "Some lonely demon out there would find him absolutely beautiful. Unfortunately, the woman is too far gone to save."

Chris frowned. "How can you tell?"

He reached down and pulled the top of the woman's shirt back to reveal the scales. "They've converged."

The other man drew his gun. "It's a shame, really. It looks like she might have been hot as hell."

In response, Damian simply shook his head and stepped back as Chris shot the demon between the eyes and watched its body turn to dust. Damian knocked the dust off his boot and put one hand on his pistol as his gaze slid over the people he had saved.

His teammate slapped him hard on the back. "That's some mighty fine exorcising there, cowboy." Damian looked slowly at the man and lifted an eyebrow. Chris cleared his throat and stood a little straighter. "I've been watching westerns lately. Black cowboys aren't common."

All Damian could do was laugh.

Across the room, Korbin twisted his body and kicked to

the side to strike a demon in the stomach. He shot almost in the same motion, killing another, and turned to eliminate the first, which now charged in earnest. Two other teammates fought on either side, focused on their own adversaries. Charlie swirled his knife and sliced through demon necks. Ethan fired his gun and looked at his partner. "What the fuck are you doing? This is definitely a gun scenario. You walked in here with a damn pocket knife!"

The other man lunged forward and stabbed a demon in the neck. "It's not a pocket knife. And I want to be the best at demon killing even when I'm not using a gun. This is the epitome of badass."

Ethan shook his head and backed up to Korbin. "You know, from the moment we started this team, I knew that one day you would bring in some idiot with nunchucks or something. Here he is, Pocketknife Charlie."

The team leader laughed. "He seems to be doing damn well with that thing. Maybe he can teach you a few things."

He scoffed. "Please. My ninja skills are on point. I got this, bro."

Korbin blasted into a group of demons and reloaded. "Just stick with your gun for now, please. I'd like us all to get back to drink some beer in one piece."

Ethan elbowed the leader and nodded to an adjacent room. "They've got the sacrifice in there. I can see them gathered around."

He nodded. "Charlie, Damian, Chris...the room over there."

Korbin and Ethan were the closest and started to fight their way through with the others close behind. The second man ran to the adjoining room and kicked a demon hard in the stomach, then slammed the butt of his gun into its forehead. Ethan dropped the empty magazine, grabbed one from his belt, and reloaded. In almost the same motion, he pulled his gun up and shot the creature right between the eyes.

A crowd of about five demons surrounded the girl. Ethan ran to the right and Korbin to the left, and Charlie came up behind them in the center. They used hand-to-hand combat at first to knock most of the beasts to the floor. The three team members fired at the fallen creatures and waited until they turned to dust.

Ethan rushed forward and untied the girl quickly. She fell into his arms, and he lowered her carefully. Charlie dropped to his knees beside her and opened his medical kit. He shined the light into her eyes. "She's not infected."

The other man pushed the blood-soaked hair from her face. "That's good, honey. You'll be okay."

The girl couldn't talk. She sputtered and gasped, her eyes wide. Charlie slapped him on the shoulder and looked meaningfully at the wound in her stomach. Her intestines actually hung out slightly. He looked at the wound and then back at the medic, who shook his head. Ethan took a deep breath and looked into the girl's eyes as he forced a smile.

He didn't really know what to say. "It's okay. Keep looking at me, sweetie. Keep looking at me. Everything will be okay."

She fixed her gaze on him and gasped for air, but her lungs filled with fluid. A small trickle of blood issued from the corner of her mouth and a long gurgling breath left her chest. Slowly, her eyes closed, and she was gone. Ethan shook her gently. "Hey, stay with me. Come on, damn it, *stay with me.*"

Charlie put his hand on his arm. "Man, she's gone."

He pushed his friend's hand away and gritted his teeth as he shook her. "God damn it, no. Fuck, *come on!*"

The medic stepped beside Korbin, and they watched as the breath caught in Ethan's throat. He released her and wiped the tears from his eyes with the back of his arm. He stood, pulled his gun, and grabbed Charlie's knife from his hand.

The team leader reached for him, but he pulled away. "Come on, man," Korbin said. "It sucks. I know. Let's finish this up and get home."

He sniffed. "*I'll* finish this shit up."

Korbin followed quickly when Ethan raced out of the room, raised his gun, and began to shoot every demon that remained. When his bullets were gone, he threw the gun aside and grabbed one by the throat, sliced its neck, and threw it to the floor. He turned, looking for more to slay. His eyes settled on the last one, a medium-sized demon that stepped from the shadows and snarled loudly.

"Oh, you want some too, motherfucker?" he yelled as he sprinted toward the beast. "Come here. I got something for you."

He ran, dropped to his knees, and slid across the floor. Beside the creature now, he slashed the knife across its legs and jumped to his feet, then slammed his fist into the demon. It roared, and a massive arm swiped out and knocked Ethan back into his teammates. He pulled away and started forward again.

Korbin reached out his hand. "Let me shoot him!"

He wiped his mouth with his free hand and gripped the knife tightly. "No, fuck that, Korbin. This bitch is mine."

He yelled his rage as he ran toward the demon and sliced his knife viciously down the front of the creature. It screeched as he reared back and jammed the knife into the underside of its chin. Ethan ripped the knife out, and blood spattered in a wide arc. The team watched as he stood with his back to them and stabbed the enemy over and over.

Finally, after several moments, the demon burst into dust. Ethan stood silently, still facing away, and hung his head. The others cheered and clapped in a show of pride at how badass he had been. The enthusiasm faltered when he swayed, and the others grew silent. He turned slowly, clutching a massive wound in his stomach. He fell to his knees and collapsed onto his back.

Korbin dropped beside him and looked at the wound before holding Ethan's gaze. "You stupid fucker."

He smiled and whispered, "I told you I was a…ninja…"

The words faded into a final rasped exhalation, and he died there on the floor. With tears streaming down his face, Korbin yelled, "*No.* God, no."

Damian made the sign of the cross and stood close beside Charlie and Chris. They remained silent as their leader mourned his fallen brother. He gripped Ethan tightly and fell back on his butt, holding the lifeless body to his chest. Korbin shook his head, his emotions etched on his face. They had been the best of friends, in it together from the beginning, and now Ethan had met his end.

All the guys knew that it could happen—and one day *would* happen—but that didn't make the loss any easier. Chris put his hand on the priest's shoulder as he began to pray, holding his bible tightly. That was the first time he had lost a family member, a teammate, and a friend to the ravages of demon warfare.

For the rest of his life, Damian would never forget Ethan's face or the way he had sacrificed his life to avenge the death of a perfect stranger.

CHAPTER ONE

The blaze crackled loudly in the firepit in a café on the outskirts of Rome. People milled through the outdoor seating area as Damian sat with a book perched on his lap. His eyes were focused on it, but his mind absorbed nothing. He was lost in his memories, as he tended to be more than ever now. No longer distracted by the constant screaming of the sirens in the barracks and the incessant voices of his teammates, he had too much time for his mind to rewind back to the old days. It wasn't healthy—he knew that—but after decades of battle, he really didn't have control over it.

Ravi cleared her throat. *Uh, Earth to the priest. What are you thinking about in there?*

He answered without thought. *Ethan.*

And who is Ethan? Don't tell me this is one of those "you joined the priesthood because of your gay lover" kind of things?

Damian cleared his throat. *No. Ethan was an old teammate. You might not remember him because you and I were not interacting much then. He was the first one I ever saw die. That was the moment I realized that none of us, and especially not me, was invincible.*

Ravi drew in a long breath. *Oh... Well, I have never been any good at this whole comforting thing. It's probably why I never became a mother. I have no patience for it. But I do know that if you ditch the coffee shit and replace it with a nice glass of whiskey, you will start to feel better in no time at all.*

He chuckled and snapped out of his reverie. *Right. I don't think they sell whiskey here.*

The demon scoffed. *I'll order you a flask.*

The priest looked around the busy streets and at the café. The people all wore their fall gear and talked happily to each other. Most carried umbrellas in case the weather turned. There were a few tourists there, but the place was so out of the way that most foreigners didn't know anything about it. All the outdoor tables were simple metal, with plastic garden chairs. Inside, the place was furnished in oak, and the colors on the wall were dark maroons and burnt oranges.

It was an incredibly low-key establishment, and Damian could see why Wally had picked it. He was very careful about where he met others, and what was said and done in public. In fact, the man was almost paranoid, but he couldn't blame him after the sheer amount of history that he had learned from his work in the catacombs beneath the Vatican.

Ravi sniffed. *Hey, where is mini-you? I thought he was coming.*

Damian put his book on the table. *No, this is information I want to see before I let him in on it. No reason to put the kid at risk if it doesn't affect him. He stayed at the hotel to sleep in and eat breakfast.*

Breakfast and sleep sound nice. Maybe you wouldn't sport so many wrinkles if you indulged a little more.

Hey, these lines are proof of how hardcore I've been through the years.

The demon sighed. *So who is this guy we're meeting?*

He took a sip of his coffee. *Wally and I met a while back. I told you that part. Anyway, he has called me several times about different artifacts, and I have called him to get some history on cases. From there, we became friends. You know, friends that send Christmas cards and call on occasion but are always there when the shit hits the fan? I feel that this one, though, might be more than a once-a-year occurrence.*

What's he like? Is he a super-godly "don't tread on my Jesus" kind of Catholic priest?

Damian chuckled into his cup. *To an extent. He's definitely devout, but he's a nervous guy, quite young, and very good at heart. He has always wanted to do what we do but knows he isn't cut out for it, so he does what he can from behind the scenes.*

She groaned. *Nervous humans are ridiculous. Seriously, besides this little war, what do you have to be nervous about? No stalking overlords, no shiny man above wanting to crush you like a bug. You have trees, birds, and good food. Oh, and fashion. He works in an underground vault. How dangerous could things be for him?*

I don't think it's so much that he's in danger as that he works around all those artifacts. He sees things that only a couple of other people ever see. I don't know everything that is down there, but he's told me about a few of them. Damian smiled as the waitress poured him another cup of coffee.

Like what? Merlin's hat? Ravi wasn't impressed.

The priest laughed. *There are a lot of possessed items— things that have been taken from exorcisms when the demon is driven out and lands in an inanimate object. It's more of a soul that lands there than a demon. The real truth is that demons don't do dolls, not really. Then there are some stones that have been proven to have demonic spiritual powers and artifacts from the time of Christ. Most of those are hush-hush. There're things that point to inaccuracies in the bible, and the Catholic Church can't have that.*

She sneered. *So, you mean the entire bible is down there? Because that thing is rife with falsehoods. Women living to be eight hundred or more years old? Pfft. Right.*

Damian realized at that moment how open and trusting he was with Ravi. It shocked him a little, but he figured there was a reason for it so he wouldn't stop. It was actually pleasant to have some sort of relationship with the being inside him. He could understand Katie's interaction with Pandora a bit better now, too.

Just then, the chair across from him was pulled out, and Wally sat down. He wore a hat, a long, buttoned-up trench coat, and a pair of dark sunglasses.

"You know that everyone is staring at you because you look like Inspector Gadget?"

The other man removed his glasses and leaned forward. "I only wanted to get out of the city in one piece."

Damian smiled and reached his hand out to shake. "Good to see you, old friend. It's been far too long."

Wally nodded nervously, and his eyes shifted constantly. "You too. You look good. I am still thrown off every time I see you without your priest get-up. They are so strict with us in the Catholic faith."

"They try to be with us, but what can they do? Fire me?" He shrugged.

His companion snorted. "They wouldn't give it a second thought where I come from."

Damian grinned. "So, how is everything?"

The other man leaned back slightly and released a deep breath. "It's been busy as hell, no pun intended. With all the incursions and openings, cult artifacts have come in from all over. Most of them are innocuous, merely kids playing at the game, but some can knock you on your behind if you aren't careful."

Ravi giggled. *Behind?*

He's a Catholic priest. He doesn't share my gift for colorful language.

"And how about the demons in the Vatican City and Rome?"

Wally shook his head and waited for the waitress to finish pouring his coffee. Once she'd walked away, he removed his hat and shrugged. "Vatican City is highly fortified, with sacred ground and blessings everywhere— even the McDonalds they recently built. We don't really see much inside the grounds. Rome is getting pretty rough, though. I've seen infected all over the place. I learned how to spot them from you."

"Yeah, the old red eyes will give them away every time." Damian snorted as he took a sip of his coffee. "Is the church helping to combat this?'

His friend swallowed and smiled his satisfaction. "Mhmm. Oh, yeah. The Catholic Church has their own coalition of mercenaries, and there are the teams that live in Rome. They are definitely getting a workout."

"I don't envy them. So, what did you bring me all the way out here for? Not that I don't enjoy having coffee with an old friend."

Wally pulled a manila envelope from his pocket and looked around before he slid it over. Damian opened it and pulled out a stack of papers. On the top were pictures of the stone his friend had mentioned. It would fit in the palm of a hand, was faceted, and glimmered with a deep red tone. Specks of black crystal-like sparkles could be seen throughout. He flipped through the pictures and read the information on where it had come from. The picture of the cardinal struck Damian, but he kept his face expressionless. It was the same straight-faced man he had seen in a picture with the three Wise Men when he'd met with them in the house down the street in London.

"What do we know about this cardinal?" He glanced at his friend, who shook his head.

"Not too much. He has always been under the radar and has never done anything to raise any eyebrows. He's an unassuming man; kept to himself but was always seen close to someone in charge. When I saw him, he gave me the impression that he was the quiet voice whispering in the ears of the most influential men in the church before stepping back into the shadows. Still, he was incredibly devout and was known to spend days fasting and praying in the main church. It really didn't make any sense to me why they would find a demon stone in his possession."

Damian raised his eyebrows and stared at the picture. "You would be surprised sometimes. These things can catch hold of you before you know it. Did he show any signs of possession or infestation?"

Wally chuckled. "No, especially not on holy ground. The man was a pillar of the Catholic community. Someone would have noticed very quickly if he had become Damned."

The priest read through the list of the cardinal's prior positions in the church. There had been a few times when he'd been sent to far-off places, but he'd always been called back to the Vatican shortly thereafter. What it didn't say was by whom. "What do we know about this vacation he went on?"

The other man sipped his coffee, a little more relaxed now. "Nothing more than that. He went on an extended vacation and left without a word. The church informed us."

Damian put the papers back in the envelope, folded it in half, stuck it in his jacket pocket, and leaned toward Wally. "I want you to find out where the cardinal went. If I know that, I can do a bit more research into this."

His friend pulled out a small pad and made some notes. "Sure thing."

He held back a smirk, seeing how excited Father Wally was to take the assignment. The man's eyes glimmered. "I always wanted to be part of the action, but you know me. I'm more of a cave-dweller than an action hero. I'm more than happy to do something that will help you uncover more about this."

Damian reached across and patted Wally's hand. "Heroes aren't only on the front lines."

This seemed to satisfy him, and he already sat taller. "There are a few artifacts down there that came in after

Incursion Day. They were among the first to be found. I'll get you some information on those as well."

"That sounds good. Wally, I seriously want you to be careful with all this. You work for the most powerful church in the world and have to worry about more than demons. The church leaders don't like it when people go snooping around or talking to others." Damian frowned to emphasize his concern.

"I know." Wally nodded agreement, his face somber. "I've seen what happens. They don't mess around when it comes to killing traitors or those who align with traitors. I'm always incredibly careful, anyway."

Damian smiled. "I know. You are probably the most careful person I've ever met."

Wally shoved his hat on. "I also don't really have any friends but you, so there isn't anyone but the mice under the Vatican to talk to, and they won't spill the beans."

"Good. Now, when you get that information, I don't want you to call me from the Vatican. I don't want you to be traced or overheard. Someone will get the wrong idea, especially if this guy has been dabbling in Satanic rituals. You must keep your hands clean with this. If I have to meet with you again in person, I will. Just say the word." Damian was serious. He didn't want to get his friend killed.

The other man pulled his phone from his pocket. "I get it. Hold on, let me take this call. *Ciao? Sì, stavo solo prendendo un caffè con un amico. Certo. Ci sarò tra venti minuti. Sì, signore.*"

He hung up and slipped the phone back into his pocket. "I have to get back. Apparently, there is a new shipment, and they need me to run some rushed tests as soon as it hits the basement floor. It didn't sound like the normal demonology studies, though. Might be another crying statue. We get those like five times a month. It's always something either man-made or which has a leak in a hollow part of the statue."

"That doesn't sound interesting in the least." Damian sipped his coffee, hiding his smile.

Wally stood and donned his glasses. "It's boring until you find something that completely stumps you. When science fails, we turn to the religious possibilities. It's probably not a method that others would recommend, but it works for the church. Sometimes, I think I'm merely there for show. They'll say whatever they like, regardless of my findings."

Damian stood and gave his friend a hug. "At least you get to work in safety. Think of the positives. Keep your ears open, and keep me in the loop about anything strange that they might talk about."

The other man tilted the brim of his hat. "Will do. I want you to do the same for me. Not only will it keep me informed, but it'll help with the research I do. I can always use that."

He smiled and watched as Wally waved and hurried off to catch a cab. Thoughtful, he sat again and ran his fingers over the pocket in his jacket holding the information. He wasn't sure what they would discover. The church was really good at hiding things, but he was beyond curious. And since Wally had now put his life on the line, he apparently was too.

CHAPTER TWO

The air was cool and the sky a vivid blue. It was a beautiful day in Rome, so Damian decided to walk back to the hotel. He pulled the papers out and began to scan the information as he walked. There was something strange but also familiar about the stones. Frustratingly, he couldn't put his finger on it. He flipped to the picture of the cardinal and studied it, noting the menacing look on the man's face but consciously trying not to read too much into it. After all, he had been the victim of several bad photographs himself.

One thing was certain—at the time the picture was taken, there was no demon inside the cardinal. Either he had been the victim of an unfortunate plot against him, or he had turned his back on the church. Either way, Damian wanted to know more about it. It wasn't something he could simply shrug off, especially after seeing him in the picture with the Wise Men.

Ravi sniffed her disdain. *Oh, hc looks pleasant.*

Damian folded the papers and put the envelope in his pocket. *I know. There has to be more to this story than it appears, though. Men of that nature don't simply turn against God. They are devout, and capable of holding back some of Lucifer's worst attacks.*

Or he was never as devout as people thought.

He shook his head. *I don't know. That is a long time to pretend and never get caught.*

Right. But if a man can be that devoted to God, what makes you think he can't be to Satan?

You're right. I'm letting my bias cloud my judgment. I'll keep an open mind on this. He released a deep sigh of irritation.

She asked after a moment, *Are you going to tell the kid?*

Damian thought about it for a second. He didn't want to keep secrets from Max, but he also knew that with some things, ignorance was safer. *No, not yet. This is very dangerous information, and we are walking on hot coals. The Catholic Church is nothing to be trifled with, and we know they're not above silencing a problem. If history has taught us anything, it's that a man will use God's name for any action if he convinces himself that it's the right thing to do.*

His demon scoffed. *That doesn't only apply to humans. I've seen my fair share of angels do that in the past too.*

Startled, he stopped walking. *What do you mean?*

She coughed nervously. *Nothing. I'm merely saying there are no perfect creatures. As far as Max is concerned, I think you're right to keep this from him.*

Damian could tell Ravi wouldn't elaborate on the angel comment. He nodded and continued toward the hotel. *I think that this is a need-to-know situation. Nothing may ever come out of it, and until it's necessary for him to be in the loop, I'll keep it under wraps.*

He entered the hotel and nodded at the front desk clerk. On his way to his room, he decided to walk next door and see Max first. The door was propped open slightly, so he knocked and walked in. He rounded the corner, stopped, and tilted his head to the side as he stared at the young priest who lay on the bed watching the Weather Channel. "Are you always the epitome of a priest? Fifty channels and you're watching the British weather station?"

The trainee shrugged and turned the volume off. "Most of the channels were in Italian, and the rest were either really bad made-for-television love stories or cooking shows. I am starving, so I decided against cooking shows, and I'm not really a romance kind of guy."

Damian looked at the screen and shook his head. "So you settled on information about London's rainy season. Isn't that all year long, unless the rain turns to snow?"

Max sat up. "It's actually pretty interesting. The prevailing warm, moist westerly winds mean that the west of the UK is more likely to receive precipitation from Atlantic weather systems in the form of frontal rainfall. These weather systems usually move from west to east across the UK, and as they do so, the amount of rainfall they deposit decreases exponentially. It even told me about—"

The priest put his hands up. "Look, Larry Sprinkle, I really don't need to know about the weather until it starts raining hellfire. At that point, you can break it down for me, okay?"

The young man smirked. "Right. Sorry. Forgot I'm the only one in the world who finds this stuff interesting."

Damian sat in one of the chairs. "You and the other weathermen of the world, spray-on hair and all."

Max laughed. "So, what did your friend need that forced you to come all the way out here?"

He looked down at his hands rather than meet his companion's gaze. "He had a crisis of conscience. We tend to call on each other when being a priest becomes difficult. It's much better to talk it over in person." His companion didn't question him, and Damian was relieved. "Our train doesn't depart until tomorrow evening. I thought we would be here longer, but it seems not. Is there anything specific you want to do while we're in Rome? I know the riveting information on the weather channel has pulled you in, but I figured I would ask."

The trainee turned and put his feet on the floor. "Actually, yeah. I'd really like to do some sightseeing. You know, the normal tourist stuff? I've never been to Rome before."

Damian tossed him his windbreaker from the chair beside him. "What does the weather say?"

Max smiled cheerfully. "Bright and sunny all day."

Damian stood and clapped his hands. "Then let's do this. I know all the spots, and I can enlighten you on some lesser-known facts about them."

"Sweet. Let's roll."

The two headed outside and grabbed a cab, and the priest instructed the driver to take them to the Colosseum. As they left the cab, the young man's eyes grew big, and he stared up at the structure as he spouted facts. "The Colosseum is an elliptical building measuring 189 meters long and 156 meters wide. It has a base area of twenty-four thousand meters squared, with a height of more than forty-eight meters. It's an impressive structure, especially since it was built so long ago. It seats around fifty thousand spectators and has thirty-six trap doors for special effects."

Damian walked up to the gate and bought two tickets. "Thank you."

Once inside, he turned to Max. "How do you remember all that information?"

Max shrugged his shoulders. "I don't know. I simply do. I retain almost everything I read. I've been like that my whole life and can picture every word I've ever read, at least when it comes to stuff I'm interested in."

The older priest was impressed. "Well, let me enlighten you about a few facts I'm positive you haven't read in a book anywhere. The builder of the Colosseum, Vespasian, was actually a fallen angel. He was still very loyal to God, but he craved a human life."

Max's face went serious. "Really?"

Damian nodded as they walked along. "Mhmm. Many of the gladiatorial combats later on in his life were, unbeknownst to him, fought against demons in both human and animal form."

The trainee's mouth dropped open. "Things make a little more sense, knowing that."

They walked into the main area, and Damian pointed to the top rows. "The back row was covered by a velarium. They said it was to block the heat, but in reality, it was to cover the angels who snuck down to see the shows with Vespasian. Right beneath our feet in the maze of tunnels is a room that was once dedicated to the demons to call for power from their master. Of course, Vespasian didn't know this. It was something his son and successor, Titus, created to calm them and ensure their loyalty in the ring. He wanted to be able to control them."

Max shook his head in amazement. "Right, so if the crowd voted to not slay the fighter, he could stop the demon from doing it anyway. And the whole time, his father was still kicking it with angels and saying his bedtime prayers. That is nuts."

Damian touched a piece of the stone. "It is. Not only that, God knew what he was doing the whole time—or at least, that was the account. He let Titus dig his own grave, knowing He couldn't step in against free will in any way. If He had let Vespasian know, He would have been breaking His own rules. Titus thought he was doing the smart thing, but actually, it was very dangerous."

They walked around for about an hour, the priest stepping back now and then so the younger man could take pictures with his phone. The kid was absolutely mesmerized. He enjoyed seeing him do something he wanted to do. Max was a good guy and was getting better at facing demons every day.

When they were done, they took a cab over to the Arch of Titus near the Colosseum. Max was spellbound once again. "Do you see the battles etched into the base? That is the sack of Jerusalem, when the city was destroyed. And there, the inscription reads, *Senatus populusque romanus divo Tito divi Vespasiani f Vespasiano Augusto.* In English, that translates to 'the Senate and People of Rome, to Divus Titus, son of Divus Vespasian, Vespasian Augustus.'"

Damian rubbed his chin as he wracked his brain. "Divus… Divus…what does that mean?"

Max looked proud to know the answer. "That means it was written after the death of Titus, and long after the death of Vespasian. If you look on the south panel, it shows Titus' triumphal march as it passed through the Porta Triumphalis bearing the spoils of Solomon's Temple. The other side is the same. You can see the menorah, the candelabra, and the oldest symbol of the Jewish faith."

Damian looked at the arch and grinned. "Are you ready for my information?" The trainee turned, his excitement palpable. "This arch was built over the top of a cult shrine to the devil. The church tried to have it removed on several occasions, but the souls surrounding it rose up in protection. Finally, exhausted from always fighting, one of the cultists infiltrated the church and had the Arch of Titus built over it. It was a distraction, and gave those who still worshipped a place to do so without repercussions for their faith."

Max's mouth twitched. "So, you're saying this isn't an actual ode to Titus?"

He wasn't sure. "I guess if you think about it, the Satanic community paid homage to Titus even though that wasn't what he wanted. They looked at him as an ally because of the way he treated the demons in the Colosseum, so yes and no. Now, though, the cultists and infected come here to feel closer to hell's gates."

Damian nodded toward a couple of tourists standing near the wall of the Arch. Their eyes were red, and they whispered something at the wall and stroked it with their hands. Max turned the other way, identifying more demons. Suddenly, they both realized that everyone around them had red eyes.

The trainee moved close to him. "I think there might be too many of them here to start a public issue."

He sighed. "I think you're right. The best thing for us to do now is simply slowly back away."

They walked slowly toward a place where Damian knew they could find a cab, trying not to look suspicious. There were too many demons, and the space was wide open. Damian made a mental note to send a merc team out there later. There were too many red eyes to look the other way.

A few blocks over, they found a cab and got out a short while later in front of a small deli and café. Once inside, Damian ordered for them both since the trainee knew zero Italian. "*Entrambi avremo il pastrami su segale con un lato delle tue fiche. Oh, e due bottiglie d'acqua. Grazie.*"

They sat at the window and waited for their food. Max smiled as a family walked past with their two young kids. "We used to take at least one summer vacation every year when I was growing up. It wasn't anything fancy. When we lived on this side of the pond, it was to see the English countryside and go to cool restaurants. When we moved to the States, though, there was a lot more to do. As a kid, I thought it was awesome. Now that I'm a little older, I realize we did all the tacky cliché vacations that everyone else does."

"Like what?" Damian wiped his mouth.

He rolled his eyes. "We went to Roswell and the tiny museum on the side of the road. We took beach trips and went to South of the Border on the way to South Carolina.

We went to Glacier National Park once, and the rest were beach and ocean. I think it was because it was relaxing for my mom too."

The older priest smiled. "I never had that chance, being an orphan. I think it's as important to see the tacky as it is to see the profound."

Max looked out the window. "I always wanted to come to Rome, and see other parts of Italy, too. I simply wanted to take everything in—see the beauty in the place. Oh, can we go to the Vatican next? I've always wanted to see it with my own eyes. I've only ever seen it in books and movies."

Damian cleared his throat, careful to keep his expression neutral. "It's extremely packed today because there's some kind of event. I think that if we tour the Vatican, we should have all day to do it. We will make another trip out here and can schedule it then. How about we go check out the Forum? It's a popular destination."

The young man looked disappointed at first but perked up after a minute or two. He launched into a recital of facts on the Forum. "The excavations to clear the Roman Forum took over a hundred years, and it wasn't until the twentieth century that it was completed."

Damian smiled and shook his head. He was simply glad that Max had accepted his excuse without rancor.

I swear, for a priest, you are like a master manipulator. Ravi laughed maniacally.

Hey, I can't have the kid watch me get arrested by Vatican Police. Not really my idea of a good ending to the trip.

Ravi sighed and finished with a giggle. *I find it funny that* I'm *the good influence here.*

CHAPTER THREE

The Forum was enjoyable, but Max was dying to see Pompeii, so they found one of the tourist buses and made the journey to view the grounds, Damian napping the whole way. When they arrived, they fell in behind the tour guide. The trainee was completely entranced by the cobblestone streets, the remains of the stone people, and the buildings all along the base of Mount Vesuvius.

He looked at his mentor, his eyes wide and bright. "The people who lived here had no idea Vesuvius was a volcano. They didn't discover the city or its remains until 1740-something. No one realized that these people were buried alive by volcanic ash. It's an insane thought. Nowadays, if a celebrity sneezes, we know about it in three seconds flat."

Damian chuckled and glanced at the tour guide. He grabbed Max's arm and pulled him away from the tour and down one of the cobblestone paths. "Do you want to know the alternate history?"

His mouth dropped open. "For this too? Cheese and Rice!"

The priest lifted an eyebrow at Max. "What?"

Max shrugged. "My way around cussing. I'll simply say random things from now on."

He rolled his eyes. "Whatever. So, the truth is, the reason the volcano became active after eighteen hundred years was that a gate opened at the base of it. The sheer power of the gate and the flood of demons coming out of it triggered the activity and blew the damn thing sky high. The people didn't die from demons, specifically, but they died from the volcano erupting due to demons."

The younger man was perplexed. He scratched his head and looked more closely at the scene. In silence, he walked ahead and studied deep gashes in the buildings. Were those from demons? As he turned the corner, he stopped and stared at an etching on the wall. Frowning, he stepped closer and rubbed his hand across the faint symbol.

He had been given a guide to demonology when he was in school. In it was a chart of all the symbols used over time to signify the devil, the cults, and the demon incursions. The leaders of the incursions—Damned humans or large demons like Moloch—often etched their symbol wherever they attacked. Max closed his eyes and flipped through the images of the symbols in his head. Near the end of the slideshow in his mind, he stopped, opened his eyes, and focused on the same symbol on the wall.

Stunned, he stepped back and shook his head, whispering, "No shit."

Damian's voice echoed from around the corner. "Ah ha! Language!" Max groaned and put his head back as the priest appeared and wagged his finger. "You can't hide from me, young student."

He ignored him, still staring at the symbol. "That is from the cultist collection of symbols."

His mentor examined it carefully. "Sure is, and it was definitely not etched recently."

They walked out onto the cobblestone streets and meandered through the visitors' area. Damian put his hands in his coat pockets, surprised they hadn't taught any of the information he had to trainees. "You know, there are a whole slew of historical events that didn't happen the way you think."

Max glanced at him, openly curious. "Like what?"

Damian wrinkled his nose and wondered where to start. "Well, the most obvious is Hitler's reign in Germany. You can see the precise moment in history that his evil went from The Count to Freddy Krueger. He was Damned, and the demon was talented enough to take over his mind and his soul while keeping his body intact. He ruled those people and killed the Jewish population to gain followers. In reality, the demon inside him didn't care who lived or died. When Hitler died, it was believed that his girlfriend Eva Braun revealed herself as an angel and took his life with the Golden Sword."

The young man looked at him in amazement. "No sh—shitake mushrooms? What else?"

The priest flashed him a side glance but hid his amusement and continued, "There is Stalin, too. It's rumored that Satan's right-hand demon at the time was in fact inside Stalin, carrying out Lucifer's wishes. In the end, he killed over six million people between mass executions, his concentration camps, and starving people to death. Even in the fifties, he was still killing Jewish people. The demon was eventually called back and left Stalin in a puddle of his own vomit."

Max shook his head. "I guess none of that really surprises me."

Damian chuckled. "Then there was the Byzantine emperor around 565, Justin II. Apparently, our good friend Moloch had come to this side and taken over his body to see what all the hype was about. He was so powerful he damaged the human, so he had servants push him around in a wheelchair, and would kill those he didn't like and have them for dinner. Apparently, he had the human chef roast them like pigs and present them at the table. He didn't like human food and wanted to feel as if he were at home. There hasn't been another instance of Moloch taking a human body since. He merely comes out in his own form."

The young man grimaced. "Wow. How did they not stop the madman? And that chef! How do you even roast an entire human body? Never mind, I don't want to know. It sounds horrible."

Damian sighed. "There have been more demon incidents in history than not. It gives me a pinch of faith in humanity. Some aren't vicious but can be entertaining—like Charles the VI, who thought he was either a wolf or made of glass. Sometimes when these demons take over they aren't able to fully take hold, and they fry the human's brains. It's rather like driving a robot with no idea where you are going."

Max looked like he might puke. "I don't understand any

of it. What about in today's society? I mean, are any of these dictators infected?"

The priest shrugged. "I don't know. Ever since Incursion Day, most have retreated and are hiding out. They won't let you close enough to figure that out. I'm sure there is some sort of connection, but then again, you must remember there are some very screwed-up people in this world, Max. Just because they are evil doesn't mean they have a demon inside them. We should be careful not to dismiss sin when we see it in others. Most likely, even without their demons, Stalin, Hitler, Justin, and Charles would still have been evil people. Many times, when someone has that predilection, the demon merely allows them to manifest the worst they already have in them with no fear. When a charismatic person is put in that position, they can do a lot of damage to the world."

Max nodded. "I guess you're right. I only wish that I could look at it and really see that we aren't as bad as we seem, you know? I don't like to lose faith in people."

"I know." Damian patted him on the back. "I hope that eventually, we can change those things. There will always be bad people, but by stopping the demons and this war, it will help considerably."

The trainee pointed to one of the last structures in the row near the back. "Let's go in there."

Damian followed him inside and looked at the pieces of pottery and carved stone tablets on the tables. In the back corner was a relic encased in glass. The plaque on the outside read, "Woman's clay mask worn as a primitive beauty regimen. Donated by the Pompeii Society, to be kept on site."

He wrinkled his forehead as he leaned forward to stare at the symbols on the mask. Placed in the center of the forehead was a red stone exactly like the one in the pictures Wally had given him. Small black crystal-like blotches floated within the stone, identical to what the cardinal had found. Symbols had been drawn on each of the cheeks as well.

The priest couldn't believe the evidence of his eyes. How could something so old have the same stone as the one found in the cardinal's room? What had the stones been used for? He couldn't help but wonder if the structure they were in had been the home of whoever had opened the portal. If so, they had sacrificed their life and those of everyone else for some sinister purpose.

He glanced at Max, who was focused on reading the informational plaque beside a layer of bones on the other side of the room. Damian slipped the folded papers from his pocket and looked at the close-up picture of the stone and the case in which it had been found. Sure enough, the painted symbols on the outside of the case almost exactly matched the ones on the mask. They were identical in many ways.

Damian wanted answers. *Ravi, does this stone or these symbols ring any bells with you?*

She sighed. *Besides the fact that it looks like the one in the picture? No. I have never seen anything like that before. There was a period of time in history when demons infused objects with power and gave them to their human followers to open portals and cause general chaos. Still, I have never heard of one actually doing more than setting off a small explosion or creating mayhem in a crowd of people.*

Interesting. Why would the cardinal have one, then?

Ravi groaned loudly. *Who knows, Sherlock? All I know is that it's hotter than a mammoth's balls in here, dusty enough to be riding a camel through this bitch, and not at all impressive. We have remains like this all over hell. Right now, what we should do is peruse the shops in Rome, buy some amazing clothes, and sip espresso at a café on the street.*

He couldn't help but smirk. She was pouting, he knew. *Come on, take in the scenery. Learn something about the planet and species that your kind is trying to exterminate.*

The demon was not enthusiastic. *First, they won't exterminate you. They'll use you as slaves. Second, I would learn about you if you would take me somewhere like a museum with air conditioning. I thought it was supposed to be almost fall. What is this hot-ass weather? I like hot, don't get me wrong, but not when I'm all balled up inside you. I'm over here trying to keep you hydrated, and you're over there worried about a creepy mask and some red stone. Get your shit together here, priest. I don't have forever. Human bodies give out pretty fast.*

Damian shook his head in silent protest. *Good to know I'm simply another body for you.*

So damn sensitive. Food. I need food and water...and whiskey. Lots of whiskey.

He brushed her demands aside. *We'll get there. Give me a second to figure all this out.*

Whatever. I'll hide in the shadow of your pancreas. Call me when it's over.

The priest jumped slightly when he felt a pinching sensation in his body. After a quick look at his companion, who was still absorbed on the other side of the room, he snapped a photo of the relic with his phone. He pulled up a confidential email and wrote a message to Wally. He tried to be as generic as possible in case someone intercepted it.

"Wally. Found this relic in Pompeii down the fourth row and all the way at the back. Look at the symbols and the stone. It looks very familiar to me. What do you think? Be in touch soon. –Damian."

"What are you doing over here?" Max asked as he appeared beside him.

"Just admiring an ancient woman's beauty routine." Damian shoved his phone into his pocket.

He put his arm around the young man's shoulder and walked him out of the structure so he wouldn't see the etched signs on the mask. He knew he would find them familiar, and that would make keeping the secret much more difficult. The young man could tell something was going on, but he didn't push for answers.

Besides, his demon was too busy yacking about history. *I can't believe he didn't bring up the most current outbreak of terrorists. It gravely affected his country, after all.*

Max was more than a little confused. *What did?*

Good Lord, kid, we need to put you back through school. I don't mean training, either. I mean elementary school. Niagara Falls was created when Lucifer came down and fought the angel Gabriel. I watched that shit from a portal. He slammed Gabriel into the ground, creating the hole, and the water was already flowing in that direction. Voila, Niagara Falls. Eventually, God sent an army and chased Lucifer back. That was the last time he attempted to walk on Earth.

The trainee glanced at his mentor. "My demon says that a battle between Gabriel and the devil created Niagara Falls. He said Lucifer slammed the angel into the ground over and over and created the hole, and the water flowed down to that point."

Damian nodded, impressed. "I'm not surprised in the least. In fact, I wouldn't be surprised if there were many seemingly natural features on Earth created by these wars. They have raged for millennia, and the battles were terrible. They still are. We now have things like skyscrapers to get in the way."

Max crossed his arms. "You know who I think is a demon?"

The priest held the young man's gaze, not sure what to expect.

"Mr. Rogers. Seriously, that man is terrifying. Or was. With the flip of his shoe, those creepy-ass puppets, and the trolley. I know that was a trolley to hell. No one will ever be able to convince me differently. He probably held cult gatherings in that freaking tree—the one with the puppet that came out."

Damian threw his head back and laughed loudly. "I applaud your imagination, but I must firmly disagree. If anything, Mr. Rogers was a literal angel trying to make the world a better place."

His pocket vibrated, and he reached in to pull out his phone. The Secretary's name flashed on the screen. He pushed Max toward one of the other structures. "Go memorize some more information while I take this phone call. And don't touch or take anything. I don't want to have to explain that to the Wise Men."

Max glared at him as he walked away. "I'm not a child."

The priest flipped his hands in dismissal and put the phone to his ear. "Well, if it isn't my favorite person whom

I know absolutely nothing about. What can I do for you on this lovely day?"

The Secretary cleared her throat, obviously holding back a laugh. "I hate to interrupt your romp through Pompeii but…"

CHAPTER FOUR

Damian looked around for any signs of a drone or a camera. "I still don't know how you do it, but it's a little creepy, sister."

She sighed. "While you're in Rome, would you like your next assignment?"

"I would not," he said plainly.

The Secretary ignored him. "Your next mission is to—"

The priest cut in. "So, do you live near me, or are you in a spaceship a light year away?"

She continued, "There is a church on the—"

"Or are you even alive? Are you actually a computer like the one in that one movie where the guy fell in love with his AI? Do you have a human boyfriend?"

The woman cleared her throat. "This parish has undergone major—"

"I'm picturing you right now as an Apple, but if I'm wrong, please forgive me. You could easily be custom-built, too. I bet you have red flashing lights on the front, and when you get angry, they get redder—"

"*Damian!*" the Secretary yelled.

He snickered. "They got redder, didn't they?"

"Are you ready to listen?" She released a deep sigh.

Damian put his thumb up in the air and waited for her response.

"Good, let's get to it then," she responded.

"Fine. What do you have for me?" He hung his head in defeat.

A suppressed chuckle now hovered beneath her crisp English tone. "There is a parish in the Italian countryside, and the leaders have been infected. We're not sure at this time if they're retrievable, but we hope they are. They've quietly turned the congregation one at a time to create something of an infected army. They're believed to actually meet at the church late at night to turn the next set of victims. Since it's the only church in a fifty-mile radius, there's a constant stream of visitors to it. Actually, they've done one hell of a job keeping it secret for this long. They still hold their services, and they even had one of the deacons from the main church attend, and he never noticed. Not surprisingly, he was captured two nights later, and we haven't heard from him since. Pictures have been taken of him at the church, so we know he's alive, but we assume he's now infected."

Damian shivered. "This gives me a creepy vibe—a *The Faculty* kind of vibe. I feel as if they're walking around like zombies, feeling fabulous and trying to recruit people into their cult."

"That's pretty much the gist of it," she replied. "We need

this stopped, and we need as many of them exorcised as possible. If you can find the head of the church, that would be fantastic. He hasn't shown his face, and the underlings have run the show. On top of that, they all have a beautiful red glow to their eyes."

The priest rubbed his chin thoughtfully. "Are you Damned? I mean, for you to know so much, you're either a computer or one of us. Well, the Wise Men aren't Damned, but I'm pretty sure they're immortal."

"Will you take this assignment?" she asked dryly.

He groaned. "Of course, we'll take the assignment, but I didn't bring any of my gear with me. Apparently, the church doesn't know what a vacation is."

The Secretary's voice went back to a business-like monotone. "You didn't take a vacation, and you shouldn't need anything other than your bible and your cross. That's how you do things with this church. We're not mercenaries, Damian, no matter how long you served on their teams."

The priest merely whistled a cheerful tune.

"Be careful with your bullets and knives, Damian," she whispered. "They see you, and you have already been warned."

Damian faked a laugh. "What? What weapons? I have no idea what you're talking about. We use force only when necessary, and in the form of our bare hands. You should see me rip a demon's head off. You'd be incredibly impressed."

"Somehow, I doubt that," she replied. "Besides, your little 'running up the side of the church' move was very popular with those watching. Acrobatics are frowned upon but not forbidden. Personally, all I saw was a showman, not a man of the cloth."

He frowned. "You are mean, you know that? You're a mean-spirited computer. Do you have settings? Because I think you need to dial back the sarcasm and push up the friendly setting at least twenty-five percent. If you are a human, then I know you worked at either the post office or the DMV before you joined the church. If not, you were that nun who smacked kids on the knuckles with rulers."

"I…can…not…compute."

The priest laughed. "Look at that. Either I broke her spirit, or I broke her hard drive. Either way, there's a teeny sense of humor in there."

The Secretary began typing, then paused. "I sent the information to your phone. An SUV will pull up. The driver will get out, and that is your car."

"How will the driver get back?" he asked.

She didn't respond. "If you need more information, you can try to ask for it. Most likely, though, I will merely send you computations from my server."

Damian shook his head with a smirk. "You're going to end up liking me. Mark my words. I grow on people."

"That's more than I can say for your choice in bowties today."

Before he could respond, she had hung up. The priest pulled the phone from his ear, pouted, and looked at the information she had sent. He shoved the device in his pocket and turned toward the structure, where Max was studying the exhibits. "I need to send some spies to figure out who that woman is," he muttered to no one in particular.

Damian ignored the two other tourists and stared at the young man, who was reading one of the informational plaques. He stopped beside him, tapped him on the shoulder, and motioned with his head to go outside. Max gave him a funny look. "Are you okay? Do you have a cramped neck?"

He rolled his eyes, grabbed the trainee by the arm, and dragged him from the building. He smiled at a couple walking by and lowered his head to whisper, "We have our next mission, a church in the Italian countryside. I have the coordinates for it. The leaders have been taken over, and are raising a creepy demon army by turning the congregation one at a time. We have to go in, free as many as we can, and attempt to find the head priest and save him as well."

The younger man looked around. "Will we take the tour bus, or—"

A blacked-out SUV pulled up, and a man in a black suit and wearing sunglasses exited. The young man stared at him, his expression disbelieving. "Really? That's *so* not suspicious."

"I didn't send him. The lady in the sky sent him."

Max was confused. "The lady in the sky?"

He shook his head. "Never mind. Come on."

Another text message came through saying that more information had been sent to a local church where a friend and priest worked. They should pick the information up from Father Trough before heading out. Damian took the keys from the driver, and they piled in. "Apparently, we need to make a stop first."

The young man looked at Pompeii with sadness. "Man,

I wanted to stay longer. But hey, I get to kick demon butt, so it's not all that bad."

"That's right. We're going to get down with it."

Ravi snorted. *Don't ever say that again. You are embarrassing me. It's like having a dad with a never-ending supply of dad jokes in my brain.*

Damian chuckled. *I got way more where that came from. Exorcise me now.*

They drove for twenty minutes and pulled up at a small church in the middle of a relatively modern town. Damian and Max got out and walked around to the back. Damian knocked on the door, and it flew open. The priest before them was in the uniform, and had wild hair that stuck out everywhere and large-rimmed glasses. He pushed the spectacles up his nose and blinked his huge magnified eyes at them.

Damian lifted his eyebrows. "Uh, Father Trough?"

He nodded and stood aside as they entered. They watched as he scurried about, taking short steps in his plain orthopedic shoes. "I have your information right here. Let me pull it from the stack. Demon hunting? Whew, that's brave. I like the basement—nice and quiet."

Slowly, the trainee turned his head toward Damian and gave him a pointed look. He smiled widely, liking Trough despite his being strange.

Astaroth groaned in Max's head. *How in all of Hades will the meatsacks beat the scale-backs in this war when they're all a bunch of weirdos?*

He pressed his lips together and tried not to laugh when Father Trough returned with a file. "Okay, yes…yes. This is the file she sent over. She said this is all you need."

Damian took the file. "Thank you, Father."

They walked to the door and turned back to see the priest whispering to himself. Damian pushed Max outside, and they hopped back into the vehicle. The older man opened the file and looked for the hours of the services. "Ah ha! Well, if we leave now, we can catch ourselves a little sermon. See what these fools are up to before we go on the attack."

"Sounds good. Been a while since I sat through a service."

Damian put the SUV in Drive. "It's in Italian."

He threw his hands up. "Of course it is. Of course."

They followed the GPS to the location and found a large number of cars parked outside. It wasn't a very big church, but Damian knew it would be filled to capacity. He turned to his companion. "This is recon. Keep your head down, and try not to look suspicious. If a red eye spots you, flash them back, so they think we're with them. Got it?"

"This is like being a CIA agent," Max said excitedly as he climbed out and followed his mentor inside.

They took their seats as the service was about to start. The main leader of the church did not come out. Instead, his second took the pulpit. Ravi groaned. *I can't believe I'm sitting through this. Seriously, aren't I supposed to be like projectile vomiting, setting things on fire, and telling a priest to fuck me?*

Damian tried to keep a straight face. *Firstly, that's a movie. Secondly, if that did happen, I would technically do it.*

Oh, no. I just got that "fuck me" thing stuck in my head. Out! Out, evil image. She shivered.

Max put his hands in his lap and glanced at the congregants. He didn't understand a word being said, because written or even spoken Latin was nothing like rapid-fire Italian. Astaroth chuckled. *Great, not only are we in a church service, but they are speaking Italian. I feel like the first three rows should be the Godfather and his people. I've never seen so many Italian demons before. Slicked-back hair is still a thing, I see.*

I feel like standing up and yelling, "Where is my cannoli?" Max suppressed a laugh.

In an Italian accent, Astaroth replied. *I'ma gonna make-a him an offer he can't-a refuse-a.*

They went back and forth until the end of the service, when Damian grabbed his arm and the two of them snuck out before anyone could talk to them. They had seen red eyes staring at them like they were fresh meat, and didn't want to blow their cover. The priest had no idea how strong any of the demons were, or if they could sense who they were.

They headed back down the road to a small village a few kilometers away. The priest parked and took his companion into a small café to have dinner and wait for nightfall. They ordered their food, and he tipped the waitress to give them some privacy.

Max leaned forward. "They'll think we're in the mob."

Damian leaned forward. "The only people who think all Italians are mobsters are white people from America. I need more information on the church."

He pulled out his phone and dialed Maps, turned on the speakerphone, and set it in the middle of the table.

She answered as she turned down her music. "Hey, Pops. You back from Rome already?"

He smiled. "You got my text."

Her gum smacked as she chewed. "Sure did. Figured you were busy so I didn't text back. What can I do for you?"

The priest took a bite of his sandwich. "I sent you a church and its coordinates, and I wondered if you could get me a layout or any information on it?"

Maps shuffled through some papers. "Yeah, I got that text. When do you need it?"

Damian chuckled. "Now, preferably, since we're about to bust up a cult."

She groaned. "I wish I could help. This place is off the map. It would take me two or three days to round up any information on it."

He nodded. "Figured it was at least worth a try."

"Yeah, sorry, Pops. Is the kid with you?"

Max lifted an eyebrow. "I'm not a kid. And I'm sitting right here."

"Pops texted me earlier and said you're making up cuss words now. What is your substitute for whore bath?" She laughed.

He didn't skip a beat. "Maps."

Both she and Damian burst out laughing. Maps clapped her hands. "Good job there, Maximus. You're getting the hang of this. You might survive us after all. You kiddies have fun. Kick a demon in the balls for me, and I'll see you when you get home."

The priest, still chuckling, leaned forward. "Be safe. Talk soon."

He clicked the phone off and looked at his companion,

impressed. "That was quick thinking, Maximus. I like it. Keep that up."

Max sighed. "It's Max. Never mind—who cares? So, what's our next move?"

Damian chewed thoughtfully and leaned back. "Well, I figured we would enjoy our delicious Italian dinner and then take a little drive back to the church when the sun goes down and see what they're up to."

The trainee thought for a second. "So, cult activity. Are we talking like goat sacrifices and blood orgies?"

His mentor laughed. "We can only hope to break that kind of party up."

Max didn't even know what to say.

CHAPTER FIVE

The team headed back toward the church but didn't go down the long gravel drive. They parked to the side and turned the lights off. The priest looked at Max and slapped him in the chest. "You ready for some reconnaissance, buddy?"

He was super-excited. "Hell…lo. Yes!"

Damian gave him a stern look.

Max laughed. "Hey, I didn't say it."

They exited the vehicle, and Damian opened the small duffel Father Trough had handed him at the last second. Inside were about a dozen bibles and nothing else. He shook his head, knowing that the Secretary'd had something to do with that one. It didn't matter. He had his cross and his bible and the skills he had picked up along the way.

He reached into his pocket and pulled on his gloves. Then he patted his inside leather pocket where his special cross always sat. "Max, I—"

The priest turned and furrowed his brow. The trainee

kicked a bush and karate-chopped the leaves. He winced and pulled his hand back when he encountered thorns. This only made him angrier, and he released a muted wail as he turned haphazardly in a circle and back-kicked the shrubbery. He looked more like a mule than a fighter, and Damian had to stifle his laughter.

He stood with his hands on his hips, letting Max get it all out of his system. He kicked and chopped, and knocked branches off the bushes and leaves all over the ground. "It looks like you've been practicing. You put a serious hurting on those bushes."

"I got skills," the young man said breathlessly as he chopped the bush again with his hands. "Astaroth has been training me hard."

His demon scoffed. *Don't you put this devastatingly embarrassing show of unsportsmanlike conduct on me. I'm a true student of the martial arts. You look like a cat stuck in a tin box. Or better yet, one of those miniature chihuahuas when you get it all riled up and set it loose.*

Max ignored the retort. He looked at Damian as he kicked his leg high and completely missed the bush. "Aren't you glad you had me train in hand to hand? Imagine if that were a demon."

The priest tilted his head to the side. "I am. What did that demon ever do to you to deserve such a horrible failure of a beatdown? I think you might distract him long enough with those moves for him to kill himself out of confusion and pity. He may take the opportunity to stab you a few times first and cut one of your legs off. Maybe both, actually."

The trainee kicked hard at the bush, but his other foot

slipped on the soft ground and sent him down onto his butt. Damian shook his head and dropped his satchel and his bible into his lap. "I think tonight maybe you should stick to exorcisms. You don't want to pull a groin muscle."

Astaroth snorted. *And every other muscle in your body.*

Max grumped and pulled the gloves from his pocket as he scrambled to his feet. He hung the satchel over his shoulder and shoved the bible into it. "I need to get, like, a super-outfit or something. I need something that gives me dexterity. Maybe like Katie's outfit."

Damian cringed, along with both demons. Ravi spoke first. *Oh, for the love of Satan, stop him!*

Astaroth laughed loudly. *I guess I should get busy growing your junk so you don't embarrass yourself.*

The priest rubbed his face in an effort to suppress his laughter. "Why don't we get through tonight, and then we can talk about it?"

Max nodded and followed him up the road. *That was rude, Astaroth. Just rude.*

Not as rude as you in a one-piece spandex suit.

The young priest caught up with Damian and looked at the horizon. "I might not be polished, but I am a lot stronger and more capable in a fight than I was on Incursion Day. I saw a lot of people killed whom I might have been able to save if I'd had this ability then. I saw your team fighting, but I couldn't join you. By the time I was infected, I had passed out."

The priest glanced at him. "Any number of things might have changed Incursion Day, but there's absolutely nothing we can do about it now. My best advice to you is to stop looking at the past. Stop thinking about what could have been done differently or what could have been done better. Living with a ghost of what might have been is far worse than living with regret. You'll drive yourself crazy with that shit. Trust me, I know. What if I had been ten steps closer? What if I had reached out and stopped my teammate when he lost his shit? He might still be alive today. The thing is, nothing can prepare you for death, and death is the one event none of us can escape."

Max nodded. "My mom used to tell me that too whenever I went through my what-ifs about school. What if I had studied harder or listened closer? She told me that the present should be my focus, with an eye toward the future. I should never forget the past because it's where I learn my lessons, but never let myself get buried in it. Accept what happened as final and concrete and move on."

Damian nodded. "Your mom sounds like a very smart lady. Kind of like me."

His companion laughed. "So, today was pretty awesome. The Colosseum is still my favorite. I think Pompeii would have been, but I had only just started sorting out fact from fiction, which is my favorite part of it. Did you know that there was a school there? I didn't know that—"

The older priest stopped suddenly and put his hand up, motioning for him to duck down. They hurried behind a low hedge and looked over the top toward the hill. Several cars were parked in front of the church, and figures walked through the front doors wearing long black hooded robes. They saw people of all ages and backgrounds, and Max recognized a few people from the service earlier.

Damian hunkered down behind the hedge and pulled at

Max to do the same. "Let's make sure they're all inside before we take a look."

The trainee gave him a thumbs-up. "Right, boss. We came at the right time."

They waited in silence for several minutes before they both straightened slowly and peered over the foliage. A man in a black robe stood in the doorway of the church and looked both ways. When he was satisfied, he closed both doors and plunged the parking lot into darkness. Damian nodded, and the two of them slunk along the hedges to the side of the building. They ducked below a window as the candles inside flickered shadows through the glass and across the lawn.

"It's amazing how this went from a sweet Italian church by day to a scary-as-shi...*Shawshank Redemption* at night," Max whispered.

Damian chuckled. "*Shawshank Redemption?* Really? That was the best you had?"

The young man shrugged. "I felt pressured. It just came out. I'm starting to think you yelling 'Language' at me is better than this. Not as fun, but less annoying."

The priest straightened slowly and peered through the window. The sanctuary was filled with black-robed people. Hanging in front of the crucifix at the front of the church was a long gray silk cloth with a pentagram painted on it in what looked like blood. About a dozen of the leaders of the church circled the front and chanted. A woman, bound and gagged, lay in the center. She trembled and watched them with pure terror. All along the altar and down the rows, black candles flickered eerily.

The sheer number of red eyes in the place cast a ruby

glaze over the room. The congregants focused on the front and chanted quietly in Italian, *"Hale, nostro padre Satana. Veniamo a te con un altro sacrificio per il nostro esercito. Ti chiamiamo attraverso le notti più buie. Portaci sangue e vittoria. Portaci i tuoi figli, il tuo respiro. Portaci morti e stanchi."*

Max narrowed his eyes. "What are they saying?"

His mentor listened intently. "Hail, our father, Satan. We come to thee with another sacrifice for our army. We call on you through the darkest of nights. Bring us blood and victory. Bring us your children, your breath. Bring us your dead and weary."

The young man shivered. "Well, that's flipping creepy."

The priest reached into his pocket and pulled out his cross. He set it on the ground and reached into the other small pocket on the opposite side. Max watched as he drew a small pistol hidden there. As the trainee pulled his gloves to make sure they were good and tight, he smiled proudly at the priest. "Hey, great minds think alike."

Max reached into his jacket pocket and pulled out the two daggers Damian had given him. He held them in the air and wiggled his eyebrows. Astaroth was already laughing, knowing the older man would have something smartass to say.

His mentor raised both eyebrows. "So, what you're saying is you're going to kick and chop them until you slip and fall, then you'll throw your knives, hoping that you at least knock one out with the handle?"

Max narrowed his eyes indignantly. "I have to say, I hit the target six times out of ten during practice. That was one of the first times I had used them, too. Give me a few weeks, and I'll be able to take a demon down from a hundred yards away with one of these bad boys. For now, they are my backup."

Damian blinked at him. "I would say it sucks that you aren't skilled enough to have my back, but right now I think it might be a blessing in disguise. I feel like if you had my back tonight, I'd end up with one of those daggers in it by accident."

His companion gasped. "I would never!"

He patted his shoulder. "Not on purpose, I'm sure. But you would definitely do it accidentally. Do me a favor and throw *away* from me. Don't try to be a hero."

Max sulked but nodded in understanding. "Where to now?"

Damian turned his attention to the window, ducked, and pressed his back against the building. He put his gun in his holster and picked up his cross. "Well, I think of it this way…why sneak in the back when you can bust in through the front doors? Give them a little shock before we take them down."

The young man clapped enthusiastically. "Hell, yeah. Beast mode commences."

The priest nodded, turned to move, then fixed his companion with a glare. Max looked at him, waiting for him to say something important. Damian patted him on the shoulder with a mocking look. "Language."

His shoulders and expression dropped as the older man chuckled to himself and strode toward the front of the building. They reached the entrance and straightened. The trainee looked at Damian with wide eyes. "Oh, please, let me do some awesome shizz and kick this door in."

His mentor chuckled. "How about we do it together? It's a big-ass door. On the count of three. One, two, *three!*"

They lifted their legs and kicked the door simultaneously as hard as they could. Both were a little shocked by the power behind their action as the door flew off its hinges and knocked out four infected in its journey down the center aisle. The ceremony ceased abruptly, and the entire congregation turned to look at them. For a long moment, silence reigned.

Damian lifted his cross into the air. "Who's up for a little exorcism, motherfuckers?"

Demons leapt from the pews, hissing defiance. The priest moved to the right, and his companion to the left. They each grabbed the first demons they saw and held their crosses in their faces. In unison, they intoned their exorcism prayer. "*Caelum Domino in die qua invocaverimus te. Hanc daemonis ad profundum inferni. Parcere animae permittere interius gratiam liberetur. Nomine Patris et Filii et Spiritus Sancti.*"

Both demons emerged from the bodies and rose into the air, where they screeched and shouted before they burst into balls of light and ash. The two men exchanged quick smiles as they moved down the aisle, systematically knocking demons down with each step. The young priest grabbed a demon off the wall and slammed him onto the floor while he shouted the exorcism. This time, he didn't wait for the creature to erupt before moving on to the next. As he progressed through them, one jumped from the pews and landed on his back.

Max pulled his knife and flipped it over in his hand to stab backward. He could feel the blade go in, and when he pulled it out, the beast fell to the floor where it wriggled and writhed until it flew back to the depths of hell. The body reformed, now dead on the floor. He tried not to look and turned away to exorcise another he held down.

On the other side of the room, Damian was a little less liberal with whom he saved. Then again, at one point he had two demons on his back and one on his leg as he exorcised a fourth. He drew his gun, shot the creature on his leg in the forehead, and pushed the body off before it burst into ash. Reaching behind him, he grabbed one of the demons from his back and held him firmly as he spoke the exorcism. The one still on his back continued to harass him, although he managed to avoid the worst blows.

Finally, when he was done, he reached back again and yanked the beast loose. "Motherfucker, I—"

The words cut off abruptly when he looked into the face of a sixteen-year-old boy taken over by hell. He blinked at him for a second, pulled his cross up, and repeated the exorcism over and over again with no success. He shook the boy hard. "Come on, kid. Fucking man up!"

Max looked across the room and saw that Damian needed some help. Otherwise, it would be his mentor's body he would carry out at the end.

CHAPTER SIX

Damian felt his emotions get the best of him as he shook the kid. He could see Ethan's face in the infected youth. Even though he knew the boy was no longer there, he could see the anguish in his eyes. On some level, he knew he had to fight himself and let go, but he was somehow stuck in a frozen tundra of emotional distress. Ravi yelled at him, but her voice sounded a million miles away. A demon jumped on his shoulders, but he didn't care. All he wanted was for the unknown boy to come back.

"Come on, kid. Don't give up." He jolted as a dagger slammed into the back of the youth's head.

He stood there frozen until the body turned to dust in his hands. As the ash cleared from the air, he saw Max on one of the pews. He hopped down and ran up to ram his elbow into the demon on Damian's back. The beast fell to the floor, and the trainee slashed his other knife across its throat.

"You okay?" he asked.

Damian swallowed and nodded. "Yeah, I'm okay. I got this."

His companion smiled. "Let's finish up then, shall we? There aren't that many left, and we need to find the leader and save his ass— I don't even have a good one for that."

The priest chuckled, snapped out of his haze, and turned to run toward a group at the front of the church. Ravi softened her tone. *You all right? I completely lost you there for a second. You froze.*

I'm fine. Just help me get this over with. He shook her off.

She smirked. *I can definitely handle that one, Pops.*

Damian threw himself into the battle. He grabbed demons, threw them down, and held his cross in their faces as he repeated the exorcism prayer over and over. Flashes of light erupted throughout the church as the infected were exorcised and left unconscious on the floor. Across the room, Max slammed his elbow into a demon's chin and knocked him unconscious.

He exorcised him and then stood, looking for the next one. Astaroth was incredibly impressed. *What you did back there for Damian took balls, kid. I like it. You are growing stronger by leaps and bounds.*

The young priest threw a demon over the pew, jumped on top of him, and yelled the prayer. *Thanks. Can we maybe talk about that later? Got like two demons left to deal with. We should be almost done.*

The demon gave Max a surge of energy. *Hell, yeah, I can do that. Let's finish this shish kebab up.*

He laughed and grabbed one of the leaders from the front and threw him into the pentagram. As he bellowed the exorcism prayer, the symbol began to shimmer and evaporate. The demon rose high and snatched at the cloth as it squirmed and writhed above Max. He grew brighter and brighter before he burst and spiraled through the dimensions into the fiery pits below.

The trainee looked around. It took a moment before he realized there weren't any more demons in the room. Slowly, Damian joined him and stuck out his hand for a fist-bump. They stood there in silence until the priest cleared his throat. "Thanks for back there. I kind of got stuck in a memory."

Max shook his head. "Don't mention it. You've done it for me. I just prayed I didn't throw a dagger into your head instead. Probably a good thing I sneezed when I threw it."

The priest's eyes grew wide, and he looked at the young priest with something close to horror.

He burst into laughter. "Just kidding, bro. You should have seen the look on your face, though."

Damian rubbed his eyes and smirked. "Where is the leader?"

The young man looked at all the people unconscious on the floor. "I didn't get him. Figured you did."

His mentor shook his head. "I don't think so. If I did, I didn't recognize him. Come on, let's look through the people to make sure. I know none of the ones we killed were him."

They hurried through the church and searched the people lying there face by face. They untied the young woman who was to have been the sacrifice and laid her on a pew. Neither was able to find the head priest. When they reached the front of the church once again, Max shook his head. "He's not here. He wasn't in the room during all this."

Damian growled his annoyance. "What should we do? Should we go looking for him? I know these weren't all the demons in the church, and he might not even have a clue what is going on. We don't need the others to find out what has happened and kill the man before we can find him."

The younger man nodded. "I definitely think he needs to be found. I seem to recall that in the file Trough gave you there was an address for the priest. He can't live far from the church. We can start at his house, and if he's not there, we can call it in and see if he went somewhere else or if he contacted any of the other parishes."

His mentor slapped him on the back. "You're getting the hang of this. I'm proud of you. You still can't cuss, though, and yes, you still have to load the heavy stuff."

Max merely blinked at him in what might have been disbelief.

Damian laughed. "Come on, that's how it goes. Don't give me that face."

He sighed and looked down at a woman sleeping on the steps. She was young and had long black hair. He wondered if her family was there with her or if she had been abducted. Luckily, none of the people there would have any recollection of the night or the terror they had gone through. They would wake up wondering why they were in the church wearing robes, and why they were sleeping there. That was the best gift they could be given.

The older man looked at his watch. "All right, we

should get over there. Who knows how many escaped from here?"

Max nodded and followed as Damian made his way to the front door. As they reached the last pew, he reached out and grabbed his mentor's shoulder. Damian turned, confused, but stopped when he held one finger to his lips and pointed at a doorway to the right.

The priest listened to the silence for several moments, figuring his companion was imagining things. He was about to speak when something clanged loudly in the basement. The team exchanged shocked glances and listened more intently. They crept quietly to the doorway.

A muffled Latin chant could be heard from below. Damian nodded at Max, who pulled one of his knives with one hand and clutched his cross in the other. The older priest drew his gun, his cross already in hand. Carefully, they descended the stone staircase, glad it made no noise. When they reached the bottom, they pressed their backs to the walls, took a deep breath, and leapt into the room, holding their weapons at the ready.

The lead priest was tied to a chair in the center of a pentagram. The four robed individuals standing around him turned and hissed at the interlopers. Their jaws were elongated and gnarled, and their eyes protruded from the sockets. They were preparing to sacrifice the priest to Lucifer and spill his blood on the floor.

"That is what nightmares are made of right there." Max shivered.

Damian grimaced. "I would have to agree with you."

The four men wore the same robes as the congregants upstairs, but their arms were so long they hung close to their ankles. Their backs were humped and misshapen, and their scaled skin poked out between the tears in the flesh of the humans they had taken. Damian looked at the younger man, and they nodded simultaneously before launching toward the demons. Max tackled one to the floor but knew there was no way he would be able to exorcise him. He wrestled with him, striving for supremacy.

The trainee stared at the demon, already wincing at what he knew would come. "Sorry about this."

He pulled his knee back and jammed it as hard as he could into his adversary's crotch. The beast wheezed a long exhalation of air from its lungs and squealed in pain. Max raised his knife and thrust it into the demon's throat. Its eyes went wide, and one eyeball fell from the semi-human face.

"Ew, gross." The young priest shuddered.

The demon exploded into ash beneath him. He reached forward and had barely snatched his dagger from the dust when a second assailant flew through the air and tackled him to the floor. The creature grabbed both his hands and held them firmly to the floor as it snarled and snapped its teeth in his face.

Astaroth saw the opportunity. *Headbutt! Headbutt!*

Max looked at the demon for a split second, then slammed his forehead into the beast's face and knocked it back. It released his hands, and he rolled onto his stomach to crawl toward the dagger on the floor that had slid just out of his reach when he was tackled. The demon snatched his leg and dragged him back, but the trainee dug his fingers into the floor and pulled hard until the tips of his fingers touched the handle of the blade.

His gloves were slippery with sweat and blood, and they slipped off. He took a deep breath and shook his head. *Sorry about this, Astaroth.*

Before his demon could prevent it, he ripped his glove off and grabbed the blade. Pain seared instantly through his hand and up his arm. He gritted his teeth and flipped over, throwing the knife at the enemy as hard as he could. It stuck in the beast's head and knocked it to the floor, where it writhed and squealed until it vanished in a cloud of ash.

Max lay on the floor, barely able to see, and clutched his hand. Astaroth had gone silent, curled up in pain inside him. Damian ran up and dropped beside him. He grabbed the front of his shirt. "Are you all right?"

Max nodded. "Just…save…the…priest."

His mentor patted him on the chest. "I got this."

Slowly, he stood and aimed his pistol. He had two shots left, and exactly two targets. Both put their claws up, and their bodies contorted. He shook his head. "Not today, Lucifer. Not today."

Calmly, he pulled the trigger and sent a bullet into each demon. They both flew back, hit the wall, and turned to ash before they slid to the floor. Damian slipped his gun back into his pocket and breathed heavily as he looked around the basement, which was now covered in dust. He turned to Max and grabbed him by the front of the shirt to lift him into a sitting position.

The priest grabbed his hand and looked at it. "You aren't cut. The pain should be subsiding."

Max wheezed. "Yep. Slowly, but yep. How's our guy?"

He turned and looked at the priest, who was half

conscious but didn't seem to have any life-threatening injuries. "He needs a doctor, but he'll be okay. Come on, let's get you up. I'll take the heavy lifting this time."

The young man groaned as he struggled to his feet and chuckled as he grasped his chest. "Is that all it takes?"

Damian smirked as he joined the priest and began to talk to him in Italian. "*Padre, adesso va tutto bene. Abbiamo salvato molti nel tuo perire. Siamo con la chiesa. Ti porteremo all'ospedale.*"

The man opened his eyes and looked at them both. "*Eroe, tu e il giovane. Tu sei i miei angeli da Dio.*"

Max leaned against the wall. "What did he say?"

He looked at his companion. "He said you are an angel from God. A hero."

The smile on the young man's face made it all worthwhile. Damian lifted the father to his feet and draped the man's arm around his shoulder. They helped him carefully up the stairs, between the unconscious bodies, and down the path to the SUV still parked on the side of the road. Max got into the passenger seat and sat, clutching his hand to his chest. The older man situated the priest, and they headed for the nearest hospital.

The staff led the priest immediately into a treatment room, and the other two men took a seat in the waiting area. Max could finally breathe again, so things had improved. "So that was a cult and not demons sent through a portal?"

"Yeah," his mentor answered. "Demons sent through the portals don't have human bodies. In some ways, they are less restrained."

"So we were probably lucky they were infected and not actual demons who don't need hosts?"

Damian shrugged. "I suppose, although I have to say, I've never seen demons like those last four. They must have been incredibly strong, and were able to contort their bodies in ways the others can't. They weren't hard to kill, though, at least when you weren't killing yourself with special metal."

Max pulled a face of fake amusement. "I guess I had to do it at one time or another. It was…kind of something that was coming, I guess. Now, I have a cool scar, and I know never to fuck with that metal again."

"And you won't look back on the past and say what if."

He pointed at his mentor. "Precisely."

Just then, the doctor stepped into the waiting room. He waved Damian over and spoke to him in Italian. "*Il tuo compagno sacerdote andrà bene. È più vecchio e piuttosto malmenato. Sta riposando comodamente ora e vorrei tenerlo durante la notte. Se tornassi domani sarebbe fantastico.*"

He nodded and turned to Max. "He will be fine. We have to come back tomorrow; he's resting."

The priest thanked the doctor, and he and the young priest headed back out to the SUV. They were more than ready to get back to their hotel in Rome. Max climbed into the passenger side, his movements still a little stiff and slow. "We are coming back tomorrow, right?"

Damian started the car. "Oh, yeah. I want to know what other hell on Earth is happening in Rome. Things look worse than I originally thought."

CHAPTER SEVEN

The drive back to the hotel was relatively quiet. It was still dark, and lights flickered along the streets of Rome. Max simply stared out the window and watched the buildings go by, and Damian thought about how he'd frozen earlier that evening. He gripped the steering wheel tightly, feeling like he had let something go that night; something that had built up in him for fourteen years.

Ravi yawned. *You know what I want to know?*

He was glad to hear her voice. *What's that, Ravi?*

I want to know why people always go to church. Like seriously, over time, I've heard the worst stories about going to church. People are molested, fires break out, and then there's the whole cult thing where people drink punch and die in a circle together. I honestly don't get it.

Damian laughed. She had a knack of telling things as she saw them. *Their faith, I suppose. That, and the church makes it a very big point to tell people it's part of their duty to attend.*

The demon was seriously perplexed. *But when they do, they almost get swallowed alive by idiotic small-time demons. Except for those last four. They were pretty badass.*

He felt sick just thinking about them. *Yeah, I wouldn't want to run into those bastards in a dark alley. They make Stephen King look like a fairytale writer.*

I don't know who Stephen King is, but if this shit is scarier, maybe I should start dictating books to you. We could be millionaires.

Damian chuckled. On some level, the dark humor of that appealed to him. *I think these people have had enough horror in their lives. I doubt they will buy horror books for a very long time.*

I seriously have a really hard time figuring out humans and their obsession with religion. I mean, they make it out to be the all-consuming focus in their lives. God will love them no matter what sect they identify with. They don't have to go to church. Life is church. In hell, we don't revere Lucifer as a god. He is more like a king, but these crazy Satanist skinbags down here treat him like a god.

The priest made a right turn, and they saw the hotel ahead. *I think part of it is that people want to know there is a bigger force out there, and they want to belong to it. Whatever they believe, whether it's good or evil, they need a creator.*

Ravi scoffed. *Crazy. Humans are nuts. Anyway, when we get back to the hotel, you know what we should do? Break into that scotch you bought while we were out sightseeing today. I think this night calls for a glass.*

I don't think I could agree with you more on that one. It has been an incredibly hard battle, and one that, surprisingly, caught me off-guard. I should definitely unwind with a glass of very good aged scotch.

His demon cheered.

When they pulled up at the hotel, they headed directly upstairs and unloaded what little gear they had. Damian hung up his trench coat and undid his bow tie and the top button of his shirt. He put his pistol in his bag, walked to the dresser, and grabbed one of the glasses. After he'd poured himself two fingers of scotch, he drew a deep breath of its deep peaty scent and released it, keeping his eyes closed for a moment. He sat, and propped his feet up on the footstool.

The evening was beautiful, and he couldn't help but notice that Max stood outside on his balcony next door, staring longingly into the night. He looked like he was mentally struggling with something. The priest knew this was a hard transition for anyone, much less someone as young as his mentee. He could remember being that young, fighting demons and doing what he had to do to survive and serve the church. While he'd always put on a tough face, late at night when he didn't think anyone was looking, he often did the same exact thing—stare out at the city.

Ravi noticed the young man too. *He looks like he needs you, Pops.*

Damian grunted as he stood and adjusted his suspenders. *Indeed, he does. It has been a long night, and those memories tend to linger. I'll go over there and see if there's something I can say to make it better.*

You'd better. That kid showed some serious balls today. He sacrificed himself and his comfort to kill that demon. Hopefully, his demon isn't giving him too hard a time over it. I suspect he's probably pissed after that kind of pain.

The priest agreed and poured another glass of scotch for Max. He figured that he would need something to soothe and calm his nerves. After all, he had been through one hell of a fight and had given it all he had. In the midst of a battle it never seemed that bad, but when you got home and the adrenaline wore off, the mental anguish of the event flooded through you. He could remember it well from when he had first become a merc.

That first battle he had experienced had almost taken him out of the running, and he hadn't had a single scratch on him. It was all the mental shit—the voices, the screams, and the look of the demon. It boiled down to how they smelled and moved. It was crazy what a body could go through physically, but even more so what one could go through mentally.

Ravi sniffed. *Hold up, hold up. I said support the kid. I did not say give away all of my valuable and delicious scotch.*

Damian laughed. *Oh, yeah? So, it's not* our *scotch? Look, the kid needs a drink. I promise that when we get back to London, I'll get you one of the bottles of scotch you wanted.*

She grumped her reluctant acquiescence. *Fine, but I know where you sleep.*

"What do you want to do when you grow up?" Max could hear his mom's voice in his head almost as clearly as when he was a boy.

"I want to travel the world," his young self had told her. "Rome, Paris, Egypt, China. You name it, I want to see it,"

He drew in a deep breath of the cool air and stared out over the city from his balcony, drawn by the twinkling lights beneath him. Rome was unlike any other place he had ever been. New York had lots of tall buildings crowded together, and everything seemed artificial. Technically, Rome was crowded too, but with all the old architecture, the cobblestone streets, and the Colosseum in the background, it felt wide open. He could almost picture the Romans of days gone by proceeding through the streets in togas on their way to the Colosseum for another rousing match.

This trip, seeing the sights and sounds, was something that he had wanted to do his entire life. He had wanted to hear the songs in his head, picture the heroes, and take in the rich history of it all. What he hadn't thought he'd do was stand on the balcony with a demon inside him while he tried to heal from grabbing a metal specifically made to kill him—or at least his demon. He'd thought it would be exciting and relaxing, but it was now filled with uneasy feelings and visions of monsters he hadn't imagined even in his dreams.

Nothing seemed extraordinary while he prayed over dead bodies and moved others, so they didn't die too. He couldn't help but think that stabbing demons in the eyeballs made for an unforgettable trip to Rome, but for one small moment, he wanted to be normal. Max wanted to experience the city like all the other tourists did. He wanted to know that when he walked around, he could notice the beauty rather than the red eyes staring back at him.

Behind him, Damian opened the door after a brisk knock and stuck his head in. He held a glass of scotch up and closed the door behind him. "I saw you standing on your balcony, so I figured I would share my spoils with you. You look like you need to destress a little bit."

Max chuckled and looked down as he leaned on the railing. "Oh, yeah? What could I possibly have to destress about? I mean, my life is just paparazzi, rich houses, and chocolate cake, right? I mean, I think those are the things people want to be able to boast about in their lives."

The priest smiled knowingly at him. "Those are some of them, although I don't think they are yours."

He turned his gaze back to the city. "No, I suppose those aren't what I want."

Damian stopped beside him and handed him the scotch. "I don't know if that is truly what anyone wants, but it sounds good on paper."

Max turned to him and looked at the glass before he tilted it back and downed it like a cheap shot at a bar. All the priest could do at that point was laugh, and he watched Max's face as he patted his chest and wheezed loudly.

Ravi grunted. *Serves him right. How dare he treat good scotch in such a disrespectful manner?*

The trainee turned, still coughing, and looked at the horizon. Damian joined him in gazing at the view. The young man was definitely right about one thing—the vista from their balcony was spectacular. He smiled at the scenery, remembering when he'd first come to Rome. "You know, I love this city."

His companion smiled. "Yeah?"

Damian nodded. "I do. I remember the first time I came here. It was about six months after I was infected, and I had a meeting with the three Wise Men and the church. I was still in the mindset of being one of God's warriors. I hated death, but I hated dictators even more. I felt that the people around me repeated history over and over again. They simply called it something else."

Max watched him intently as he talked. "That's funny. They always say Americans learn from their mistakes."

The priest scoffed and took a slow sip of his whiskey. "Please. The United States struggles with knowing the difference between moral obligation and what is best for the top rung of people. Anyway, I ended up with a very old priest, who told me a story about a boy who had a really bad temper. His father gave him a bag of nails and a hammer and told him that every time he lost his temper, he had to hammer a nail into the back fence. The first day was the worst; he knocked in over thirty nails. But over time, that number decreased because he learned how to control his emotions."

Damian sipped his scotch. He could almost hear the old man's voice in his ear.

"For every day that he nailed no nails into the fence, he could take one out. After thirty days, he was able to go to his father and tell him he'd removed the last nail. His father took him out to the fence and said, 'You have done well, my son, but look at the holes. The fence will never be the same. When you say things in anger, they leave a scar just like this. You can put a knife in a man and draw it out. It won't matter how many times you say, 'I'm sorry.' The wound is still there.'"

Max smirked a little and shifted his attention to the ground far below. "So you learned that the way you treated people affected them long after the physical evidence was gone?"

His mentor pointed at him. "Yep. Exactly. And I made a vow to myself that I would do whatever I could to protect people from there on out. Anger, frustration, hurt? They're almost always justified but seldom accomplish anything. That right there was learned through generations of watching other men's mistakes. Sitting in the light of the moon with the quiet streets of Rome below me, I fell in love with the place. It wasn't for its grandeur or history. It was for its lessons in humanity."

The young priest breathed deeply and closed his eyes. "I still struggle with the fact that we can't save everyone. God, I know it sounds juvenile and ridiculous, but that's what goes through my mind. I hate to say it, but I think it's unfair. These people were Damned because they were in the wrong place at the wrong time. What kind of divine justice is that?"

Damian nodded thoughtfully before speaking. "Well, I don't necessarily agree with the church on that aspect of it. I believe that the infected soul is fought for by the angels. That a person infected by a demon unknowingly or unwillingly is not punished by God. I also don't believe that they are banished to the gates of hell. Instead, I think that just as the bad are turned away from heaven, the good are turned away from hell. The true soul and spirit aren't wanted in the fiery abyss below. They're too strong for it."

"So where do they go?"

He shrugged and turned to face his companion. "Wherever God wills them to. I think they're judged on the soul they had before they were Damned. They are judged based on their dedication to their maker and the kind of life they led while they were here on Earth. It's that simple."

Max smiled. "That makes a lot more sense."

Damian gave him a half-grin and patted him on the shoulder as he walked toward the door. "Relax for the evening, and simply enjoy being in Rome for one last night."

The priest left the room and returned to his, hoping that he'd helped the young man in one way or another. He wanted him to be comfortable with his choices and beliefs, not torture himself for not being able to save everyone. He sat in his chair again and pulled out the envelope Wally had given him at the beginning of the day. It was time to see if he was right about the artifact in Pompeii. If he was, he needed to figure out what the hell was going on all over the Earth and where those stones had come from.

CHAPTER EIGHT

Max threw his towel over his shoulder as he exited the elevator and walked down the hall. The smell of chlorine filled his nose as he reached the door of the indoor pool. He looked around the large room, happy to find it completely empty. The warm air enveloped him like a blanket and relaxed his tensed nerves. He wanted peace and quiet, and he'd figured he would find it there since it was so late at night. The floor was wet from the guests earlier in the evening, and his flip-flops squeaked across the tile floor.

He walked to the farthest pool chair and tossed his towel over the back. Grasping his wrists, he twisted his tired, sore muscles back and forth to loosen his body. He had forgotten what it was like to not have Astaroth to heal him, but he assumed his demon was either angry or recovering from the blowback of grabbing that dagger.

The young priest slipped his sandals off and covered his eyes with the goggles he'd hung around his neck. He walked carefully to the edge of the pool and sat to slide his legs in first. The pool was a surprisingly comfortable temperature, and he slipped the rest of the way in. He dunked his head under the water and squeezed the air out of his goggles, then gripped the coping and pushed off hard. Instinct clicked in immediately, and he dropped his face into the water as he pumped his arms in rhythmic strokes. He swam as fast as he could, and when he reached the other side, he turned and pushed off again. While he wanted to work his body, it was more important to strip the rampant thoughts from his mind. He had prayed until he was blue in the face, but he knew that God wanted him to work it out on his own.

After about five laps, he stopped in the deep end and removed his goggles. He tossed them up on the deck and dipped his head back into the water. Despite his labored breathing, it felt good. His body had loosened, and for the moment, his mind was quiet. It was exactly the effect he had set out to achieve. He needed the silence in order to get things straight in his head.

Astaroth cleared his throat. *You know, if you don't slow down, you'll end up drowning in a pool in the middle of Rome. Now I have to admit, that's better than at the hands of another demon, but it's not exactly how I saw myself going down.*

Max was relieved to hear his voice. *How are you feeling?*

The demon groaned. *I've been better, that's for sure. That metal hit me like a freight train.*

I know. That was rough. I'm sorry.

He sighed. *I'm not mad at ya, kid. You saved our lives. You would have been dead, and I would have been back in hell. I think I like this life a little better than the other one.*

The young priest smiled, turned on his back, and pushed away from the wall. He floated and stared up at the reflections on the ceiling. The water cast shadows there and reminded him of when he was a kid, sitting beside his parents' pool late at night as he watched the ripples shadow the ground under the moonlight. The sensation calmed him, and he almost felt like he could float there forever. He wondered if that was what death would be like.

Max thought about his demon and how far the two of them had come since he was infected on Incursion Day. Initially, they hadn't spoken to one another at all, much less had meaningful conversations. He knew it was a demon, but he didn't mind the company. *You know, after all this time, I really don't know a lot about you. I know that you've been in several human bodies before and seen a whole lot of really cool history with your own eyes, but nothing else. What do you like to do? What are your interests and hobbies when you are in a human body?*

Astaroth was slightly taken aback by the question. *I don't think I've ever had my host ask about me. Either they are so weak-minded that I take them over almost immediately, or they only care about what they can get by having me inside them.*

The priest swished his arms through the water. *Well, welcome to this lifetime in this human body. Neither of those is me.*

The demon thought about it for a moment. *I know one thing. Two lives ago, I started drinking coffee. It was the time of Copernicus, when you could walk into a Roman coffee shop and talk about life. You could debate the big questions of the universe. You could come from any walk of life, and no one judged you inside those walls. I tried all kinds of different coffees and wound* up absolutely loving the taste. *In the next life, I traveled around testing beans and enjoying coffee all over the world.*

Max chuckled. *That is a crazy life. I can't even imagine it. I have to tell you, they've figured out that too much coffee is bad for you. The caffeine is bad for your heart. Plus, the stuff you add to it is bad for your body. They say one cup a day is okay, but more than that and you simply pump crap into yourself.*

Astaroth scoffed. *Please. I will live forever, remember? I know I should care about my human body, but come on. I'm still a demon. Lavender ice cream isn't good for you, either. It's sugar and flavoring and milk, but I definitely won't give that up.*

He knew he had a point. *Yeah, I won't give that up either. What else?*

The demon chuckled. *Okay, there are some hobbies that I have really enjoyed before, but they are pretty out there.*

Max liked the sound of that. *Yes. That's what I'm talking about. What are they?*

He took a deep breath. *Okay, so the last body I was in, he was a farm boy. Straight-up plaid-wearing ride-my-tractor tend-my-cows farm boy, so I started doing what* he *did for fun. He was a competitive mooer.*

Max's face went blank. *A what?*

A mooer. You compete in mooing competitions. I would stand in a field—or my human would, at any rate—and we would fucking call the cows home. We won like sixteen competitions. Then there was soap carving, which sounds boring, but I made some pretty amazing pieces.

The man tried not to laugh. *That sounds like it's along the lines of basket weaving.*

Probably is, but hey, I like it. Then there was the weirdest one, but it really calmed me. It was called Hikaru Dorodango.

What the hell is that?

Astaroth chuckled. *It's polishing dirt. Seriously, that's what it boils down to. You take a ball of mud and draw the moisture out of it while you coat it with finer and finer layers of soil. After that, you work the dirt by polishing it into a sphere by hand. They come out looking like balls of marble. It's cooler than it sounds.*

Max laughed. *I sure hope so.*

The demon shrugged. *I also went through a serious hooker phase, but it got boring and expensive, so I decided that dating was cheaper. With you, I don't have to worry about either. I'm okay with that.*

He shook his head. *That's good, since I'm a priest.*

How about you? And I don't want some dumb answer like you didn't have any. Humans have this weird obsession with always staying busy.

Max thought about it for a minute and decided why the hell not? *Well, during my early teens, when I wasn't infected or fighting demons—before I even knew there was a war going on with the demons—I was part of a Dungeons and Dragons group.*

Astaroth was silent for a moment and then burst into loud laughter. The priest scowled and immediately regretted the admission. It was always something he got shit for, and apparently, his demon was no exception. *Yeah, yeah, laugh it up.*

He sounded like he was crying, he was laughing so hard. *Oh, God, were you like a monk in that game? Or did you lust over the sexy D&D characters? Oh, holy hell. I can't stop laughing. I can see you now with a black Dungeons t-shirt, braces, glasses, and your nerdy friends arguing over the eight-sided dice.*

Max groaned as he floated, not quite as relaxed as before. *You're a real dick, and you know what? You were in mooing competitions and polished balls of dirt. I don't think you have any room to talk.*

No, I do. You are the ultimate nerd.

Damian returned his chair after he'd retrieved an envelope from the front desk. Apparently, Wally had stopped by at some point and left it for him. He pulled the pictures out and flipped through them. They showed a plethora of different artifacts, some from the Incursion and others dated after that time. These were the pieces Wally had said he would get to Damian to study.

The first photo showed a rather plain-looking vase, but when he used a magnifying glass to better see the design, it showed rows and rows of etched symbols that belonged to different Satanic groups around the world. On the bottom were initials, but they were so badly scratched that Damian couldn't make them out. He continued through the pictures, finding several of the red stones attached to different items, including a small tabletop and a tiara, and another loose one. There were also several stone tablets etched with symbols instead of written words. Next were small glass vials with liquids in them. The strangest part was that some were dated decades before and yet they were still full.

The last few pictures displayed dozens of necklaces laid out on velvet cloths. Every one of them had the same symbol etched into the exterior of the charm. All were virtually identical.

Damian studied the information sheets, but they didn't provide much detail. He flipped back to the charms and studied them more closely, shaking his head. The symbol looked so familiar. He grabbed his phone, opened the picture he'd taken in Pompeii, and held the image of the charm next to that of the artifact he'd seen. The symbol etched into the Pompeii mask was the same as that on the charms and several other objects Wally had sent pictures of.

He leaned back in his chair, confused. From the information sheets, it seemed that all the artifacts were from different times. Some of them dated back decades, and others only a few years. He had no idea what it meant for them to have a symbol matching the artifact from Pompeii, other than that whoever these people were, they dated far back in history. How in the world could something that powerful stay so strong for so many years without anyone in the church knowing about it?

Either someone *did* know but kept everyone else in the dark, or this cult was incredibly good at hiding themselves, even in the face of mass destruction such as Vesuvius or the many other abhorrent events throughout history that had to do with cult activity. If the cardinal had possessed the symbol or the stone, then he must have understood exactly what they were for.

Ravi was paying close attention, even though Damian hadn't noticed. *Can you take that third picture out again? I want to have a closer look at it.*

He was surprised. *Did it look familiar to you? None of these things make much sense to me.*

The demon wasn't sure. *I don't know. There are so many different things here on Earth. Some are attached to hell, and others are human creations they want. This may be no different, but I want to be sure about it.*

Damian flipped through the pictures again and pulled out the one she'd requested. He leaned forward and set it on the footstool in front of him. Thoughtful now, he put his elbows on his knees and pressed his hands to his mouth as he studied it once more. It was a large leather-bound book, although he couldn't tell what type of skin had been used. It didn't look like cow, but it was very old and Damian was no expert in animal hide.

On the cover, a large symbol had been burned into the leather, although it was different from the others. It was large, didn't have the sign of Lucifer in it, and curved more whimsically. He gave Ravi some time to study it and waited impatiently for her to say something—anything. Recently, she had tried very hard to help him solve mysteries and answer the questions he had about demons, fallen angels, and everything that went on inside the church.

The two of them had gotten pretty good at connecting the information dots, and sometimes they felt like a pretty good team. After a few minutes, though, he couldn't wait. *Ravi, what's going on?*

She took a deep breath. *That symbol...I think I've seen it before. It looks really, really familiar. I haven't seen it in a century, so I want to make sure that it's actually the symbol I'm thinking of before I tell you about it. If I get it wrong, it could be bad for you, and for Wally, too. This is really sensitive stuff, so I think being cautious is good. A lot of symbols look similar, and I don't want to give you false information.*

Damian understood. *No, that's fine. I don't want you to give me wrong information either. We will do some research, and then you can decide whether it's the one you're thinking of or not.*

He stared long and hard at the picture. There was something about the symbol that caught his attention too. It was like he had seen it somewhere before, but he couldn't put his finger on where. Whatever it was, it didn't give him a good feeling in his chest. He had seen a lot of bad things when it came to cults, and he really hoped this wouldn't be one of them.

CHAPTER NINE

Damian groaned, rolled over, and slapped the alarm clock. It had vibrated in his ear for about twenty minutes. He was usually on top of mornings, but only because he rarely slept through the night. The previous evening, he'd had no problems staying asleep but rather with keeping the nightmares away. He had dreamt about old times—about Katie, and about losing Ethan. Somehow, the symbols he had found and what they could mean for the world invaded his dreams, too. Lastly, he dreamt about Max standing in a room with the three Wise Men around him. He called to Damian, but he couldn't move. His hands and legs were shackled, and sounds of screeches and yelps echoed from below the ground.

When the alarm went off, it jolted him from the nightmare, but when he opened his eyes, the sun blazed brightly in his face. He wasn't ready to face the day, something he knew was indicative of his struggles. Ravi yawned and sniffed. *You gonna get up, or do I have to take your body over* enough to walk you out of here like a zombie? I don't have any experience working human bodies so it might not be pretty. I can't control bowel movements, drool, and walk you at the same time.

He groaned and flopped onto his back. *I was up late last night. I couldn't sleep with those symbols floating around in my head. I know I've seen them before. And with you feeling that they were familiar, I was done for. When I finally fell asleep, the nightmares were ridiculous.*

She scoffed. *Trust me, I know. I couldn't sleep because of the anxiety building up inside you. I tried to wake you, but you were out. Luckily, I ride around in here, so I don't really need to do any heavy lifting.*

Damian pulled the covers up. *Let's hope not, at least for one day.*

Ravi sent a surge of comfort through him. *What did you end up figuring out last night?*

The priest sat up and leaned against the headboard. *Nothing, really. There isn't a lot of information online about that stuff. I ended up scanning it and sending it over to Maps. She can find almost anything.*

The demon chuckled. *Yeah, I like that human. She's got it down. Very resourceful and spunky, although I don't think she and I would have anything in common if I took her body over. She would have me dressed in fishnets.*

Fishnets are worse than bowties? He smirked.

She thought about that for a minute. *I'll have to get back to you on that one. At least you're comfortable most all the time. I don't have to worry about your ass cheeks hanging out the back of your pants. I'm a fashion girl, but I'm also relatively modest when it comes to stuff like that.*

Damian pursed his lips. *That surprises me, but I like it.*

She chuckled. *Get out of bed, Pops. It's time to pack up and get out of Rome.*

The priest sneered, dragged himself out of bed, and stretched his arms over his head. He glanced out the window at the Roman scenery and smiled. It was definitely a beautiful thing to see first thing in the morning. London had its charms, but for security purposes, there was no awesome view from where he lived. They had explained to him when he had first moved in that there was a reason he was stuck off the beaten path. It made it harder for demons to track him down.

He pulled out his last set of clean clothes, dressed, and finished packing his things. When he was done, he glanced at Max's balcony but figured he was still sleeping. He would likely throw on his wrinkled priest getup and rush out the door. That was one thing about Damian that wasn't at all like his trainee. He had always been prim and pressed, even before being infected.

Damian walked to his colleague's door and knocked. To his surprise, it opened immediately. Max left it open. "Morning, brave Yoda. What's the plan for today?"

The older man stepped inside and looked around. Max was dressed in a clean and ironed uniform, the coffee had been made in the small pot in his room, and his suitcases were all packed and ready to go. They were stacked neatly in the corner by the door, and he had even taken the time to make his bed.

He handed a hot cup of coffee to his mentor. For once, the priest didn't know what to say. He looked at it for a moment and set it down, thinking it was a trick. Surely the young man's things were still strewn haphazardly around the room. He glanced in an open drawer, but it was empty, and the bathroom had been tidied. Max chuckled. "You okay? Looking for someone hiding in the curtains?"

Damian gave him a "yeah, right" look. "I know you better than that, young man. No, I have to admit, I'm very surprised that you're already up and completely prepared for the day. I expected to have to roll you out onto the floor."

His companion laughed and finished his coffee. "Hey, *somebody* has to have their shit together around here." The priest raised his eyebrows, but he lifted a hand to stop him. "I know, I know…language!"

The older man pursed his lips and nodded, the opportunity to reprimand Max well and truly gone. "At least I don't have to repeat myself. You do that for me."

Max shrugged. "Add it to the list of duties I am to perform for you, oh great prophet."

Damian threw his head back and laughed loudly. "I think I would be passed over for that job."

The younger man smiled. "You ready to get going? I asked the front desk to pull the SUV out front so we could load up quickly."

Now he was impressed. "Yep. Let's haul our luggage down, then."

His companion cleared his throat and nodded toward the door. A luggage cart stood there, all ready for them. He gave Max a thumbs-up and took one last look around the room before he headed to his room for his stuff. They piled the baggage onto the cart, and the trainee pushed it toward the elevator. Damian closed the door, and he patted his pocket quickly to make sure he had his cross.

When they got downstairs, the car was open and ready, and it took only a few minutes to load up and head out. They took the same route they had used the night before and pulled up in front of the hospital. In a few minutes, they had checked in at the front desk and headed to the priest's room.

As they entered, the man looked up from the paper he was reading in his bed and stared over his glasses. A smile brightened his face. "Ah. My saviors. Damian and Max, right?"

Damian stepped forward to shake the priest's hand. "You speak English."

He chuckled. "I am from Forks, Washington. Father Richards is my name."

"Good to meet you, and it looks like you are feeling much better."

Father Richards folded his paper. "I am, thank you. I was about to get dressed and break out of here—with the doctor's permission, that is."

Max approached. "Father, we have to go back to London today, but we were hoping to ask you a few questions about what happened."

He nodded. "Of course, though after the bump on my head, I'm not sure how much I will really remember."

Damian shook his head. "No problem. I guess the first question I have is how the demons were able to infiltrate the church when it is a holy place. For centuries, it has been known that their power isn't strong on holy ground."

The priest cleared his throat and frowned. "I'm afraid

that has to do with history. The church was never blessed. It was built by the townspeople decades ago and run as an offshoot of the head church. It wasn't until the eighties that we had representatives like me there."

That explained a lot of things. "I see. Then you had a couple of bad seeds, and they kind of sprouted within the congregation."

Father Richards stood up and pulled his pants on under his hospital gown. "Precisely. Once they had infected my other priests, it was too late to do anything. I sent a letter to the church but waited quite a while for a response. By that point, we were already overrun."

Damian sighed. "I'm sorry for that. We did our best to exorcise whoever we could. The rest, unfortunately, were beyond help."

He buttoned his black shirt and patted Damian on the shoulder. "It's all in God's hands, anyway. Nonetheless, I owe the two of you my deepest and most sincere thanks for not only saving me but the majority of my congregation. I'm glad you told me they won't have memories about what happened."

Just then, the door opened, and one of the kids Max had exorcised walked into the room and smiled at everyone. "Father, are you ready to leave?"

Father Richards buttoned down his shirt collar. "That I am, young man. How are you feeling after that gas leak?"

The boy rubbed his head. "Okay. I'm still not sure how I ended up at the church so late, but if you're going to be injured, I guess that's not a terrible place to be."

He glanced at Max and Damian and hesitated as if he recognized them. The priest pointed to the floor by the door. "That's my bag, which I asked to be brought to me this morning. Would you take that outside? I will meet you there. These fine gentlemen can walk me out."

The youngster nodded, grabbed the bag, and looked at the visitors one last time before he left. They walked the priest out and shook his hand.

"Good luck, boys," Father Richards said as he entered the car. "You're doing a great service for the church."

Damian patted Max on the back. "Come on. We have enough time before our flight to grab some food."

The younger man looked strangely at him. "I thought we were taking the train back."

He shook his head as they approached the SUV. "I didn't want to deal with bouncing around for hours and figured you wouldn't mind a plane ride."

They headed to the airport and directly to the bar. A table was available, and the waitress took their orders. The older priest had already grabbed a drink, and his companion skimmed the menu. "I'll have a *Porchetta di Ariccia* sandwich and an espresso, please."

She smiled and left. Damian raised an eyebrow. "An espresso?"

Max shrugged and put his napkin in his lap. "My demon's favorite thing is coffee, so I decided I would give it a shot. He has studied coffee through the centuries. I figure if it's good enough to hold his attention for that long, I might as well give it a go."

The priest laughed. "At least our demons have good taste in drinks."

"Oh, yeah? What does your demon enjoy?"

He held up his half-glass of top-shelf scotch. "Would you expect anything different from a demon inside me?"

Max simply laughed. Ravi sniffed. *I like this stuff. Still not as good as that reserve bottle you brought home a couple of weeks ago, but it'll do in a pinch. But please don't order any on the plane. Their mini bottles are the pits.*

The trainee enjoyed his lunch, and when they boarded their plane to London, he took the window seat. Damian leaned his chair back and opened his laptop. He didn't even have a chance to talk to Max before the young priest was asleep, his head on a pillow pressed against the window. With a fond smile, he pulled a blanket over Max and focused on his laptop. The strange symbols still teased his brain, and since he was no longer exhausted, he could use the travel time to try to find more information.

He searched through pages and pages of old cult symbols from London and other parts of the world, but nothing caught his eye, and his frustration mounted. He skimmed the last page and reached up to shut his laptop, but stopped when something grabbed his attention. The symbol from the artifacts was displayed in the final entry. He read the explanation aloud in a hushed whisper. "This symbol, although it has existed for centuries, is now used mostly in the United States by elitist cult organizations residing primarily on the East Coast."

At that moment, a light bulb flashed in his head, and Damian remembered exactly where he had seen it before. Years before, he had gone on an incursion call with Korbin's Killers as part of a multi-team assignment in Washington D.C. They hardly ever worked there, but help was needed for a big case. He had fought long and hard that day, and when it was all over and the ash had cleared, two Supreme Court Justices were in handcuffs, waiting to be sent to research.

"These assholes have given us hell for weeks," one of the local mercs had told Korbin and Damian.

He had walked to the altar and looked at the floor below it. The symbol had been painted on the ground, circled in red, and was surrounded by melting candles. Even now, he could remember it vividly despite the thin layer of dust that had coated it.

After he had taken a picture for historical reference, he picked up one of the cloaks that had been worn by a demon he had personally eliminated. It was a long shimmering black-hooded garment with the same symbol embroidered on the breast. Korbin had walked over and looked at it over his shoulder.

Damian glanced back at him. "Mean anything to you?"

The other man shrugged. "Another cult, another symbol, although that's an old one. It had ties to Pompeii and several other incidents. They're always officials of some sort, and they're all willing to sacrifice for the cause. Except for these two assholes, of course. They were in it for the money and the power."

The Fasten Seatbelt sign dinged above him, pulling him from the memory. He knew that there was something more to it than his mind playing tricks on him. That symbol was obviously used by that particular cult, but the group had enclaves all over the world. It was a sign of doom—or at least appeared to be such—and Damian wondered if they had begun to gather once again.

CHAPTER TEN

It was late afternoon by the time the duo pulled up in front of the iron gate of their house in a cab. They retrieved their luggage and paid the driver before Damian unlatched the gate. Max elbowed him with a fake smile plastered on his face. "Incoming."

The priest looked up to see Rose standing in the court-yard with her broom. As she waved at them, her eyes flashed between red and brown. "Yoo-hoo, boys. I'm so glad you're home safe."

They walked up the cobblestone path toward her, and she set the broom down and held up a finger. "Hold on one second. I have something for you."

She ran into the house and returned quickly, carrying a fresh apple pie. The men exchanged glances, and the older man took it from her. "Thank you so much, Rose."

Damian set it down on the patio table. He could feel the warmth of the pie through the tin plate. He put one hand in his pocket and eased the bag strap on his shoulder. "How has the weather been?"

Rose glanced strangely at their house and again at him with a smirk. "Oh, it's been lovely here. Barely any rain. Where did you guys go off to? More work with the church?"

He patted his bag. "Nope. Merely a nice relaxing touristy trip to Rome for a couple of days."

Max nodded. "We saw all the sights except for the Vatican. There was an event, and we wouldn't have been able to get in."

The woman wrinkled her nose and scoffed. "The Vatican? Not as impressive as they make it look on television, that's my opinion. The Catholic Church has some learning to do. All the rosaries and puffs of white smoke in the world won't get you into heaven if you're weak at heart. Damn Catholics can't seem to get it through their heads that God is watching them and their sin."

Damian observed her face as Max looked awkwardly around the courtyard. Her eyes flashed red and back to brown as if she were fighting her demon. The priest stepped forward and leaned closer to her. "You know, I might be of assistance with your…little problem. Just let me know."

She laughed merrily. "If you're talking about the rats in these old homes, no one is able to handle that. Other than that, I have no idea what you're talking about."

He gave her a knowing smile and stepped away. "Well, we have some unpacking to do. Thank you for the pie. And put up your feet. You deserve it."

Rose giggled. Her eyes deepened to brown, showing her

true persona for a moment. As they walked toward the side gate that led to the garage, Damian could hear her snicker and hiss to herself. Some of the whispers were light, but others sounded dark and demonic. It was obvious that she was arguing with her demon. Max carried the pie happily as if he'd noticed nothing.

They entered through the small door to the right of the garage and set their bags down on the workbench. The trainee retrieved the key to the large lock on the armory closet Damian had installed before they left and unloaded the few weapons they had taken. "I thought I would be sad to leave Rome, but I'm really happy to be back. It's starting to feel like home here."

Damian inserted a fresh magazine into his pistol and handed it to his companion, who put it in the closet without so much as a glance before he locked the large doors and handed the key to his mentor.

"I'm glad to hear that. It's important for us to feel at home. We could be here for a very long time. You must have a sanctuary to come back to after the things we deal with, or you'll go nuts. In the barracks with the mercs, they always gave me space to set up a small church. It was *my* sanctuary."

Max indicated the neon cross in the corner. "Was *that* part of it?"

The priest smiled, recalling how it had added light to the dark room at the base. "Yep. It has been in three different barracks and is still going strong. What will you do with the rest of your day?"

His assistant slung his backpack over his shoulder. "I'll unpack, change, and head into town. There's a café where I can get samples of coffee from all over the world to try. I've been told they have the best selection."

"I know the place, and maybe I'll join you. There's a shop near there where I can buy some specific whiskeys. My demon has a list a mile long, and I'm afraid that if I don't start indulging her, she might revolt."

Ravi snorted. *Damn straight, Pops. And let me tell you, you totally have me excited right now. It's like New York Fashion Week, but for whiskey. Now I know what those kids feel like when it's Christmas Eve and they wait for their parents to lie to them and put presents under the tree from a fake fat man in a red suit.*

Damian chuckled. *Man, you sure know how to ruin a good thing.*

Please, like you don't think that's weird? I— Wait. What is that? Something isn't right.

The priest immediately reached out, grabbed Max by the arm, and put his finger to his lips. Moving quickly but stealthily, he opened the cabinet again and snatched his pistol. He closed the cabinet carefully and walked toward the door to the house. His companion pointed at the broken lock. The door stood ajar. Barely an inch, but it was obvious that someone had broken in.

Damian pushed Max behind him and held the gun at the ready as he pushed the door open slowly. The house was dark, all the windows covered by thick drapes. He squinted into the shadowy hall and stepped forward with Max close behind. They crept down the hall and into the entryway, where a staircase stood. He aimed the gun up the stairs, shook his head, and looked toward the living room.

The flicker of the fire cast shadows on the section of

floor visible through the doorway. Nothing else seemed to be out of place, so Damian assumed whoever was in there wanted something other than their possessions. Carefully, they edged forward, and the priest drew in a deep, quiet breath. He raised his gun and flung himself around the corner, the barrel aimed directly in front of him.

His eyes were still adjusting to the light, and he blinked several times at the shadow of a man on the wall above the fireplace. He opened his mouth to issue a challenge but stopped when the visitor cleared his throat.

"Do you know that you have a neighbor who's a demon?"

He reached over and clicked on the standing light as he exhaled a deep breath of relief. His old friend Abraham sat in a comfortable chair, his legs crossed before him as he absorbed the heat of the fire. Max stepped out from behind his mentor and glanced from one man to the other. He barely registered the stranger, thoroughly distracted by the fact that the man knew Rose was infected.

He turned to his mentor. "What does he mean? Is he talking about Rose?"

The priest sighed and patted him on the shoulder. "We can talk about it all later. Why don't you put the pie on the table and go change your clothes? It looks like I have an unexpected visitor to entertain."

The trainee narrowed his eyes at him; he obviously had more questions. Damian's gaze darted to the visitor, who stood now and wiped his palms on his dirty gray jeans. Max had no idea what the hell was going on, but he gathered that it wasn't the time to ask more questions. He took his bags and turned to find the stranger standing there with his hand out.

He put the pie on the table and shook his hand. The black goatee and long black hair made him look like some foul villain from Harry Potter. "Nice to meet you. I'm Abraham, a long-time friend of Damian here."

Max nodded. "I'm Max. Damian is my mentor."

Abraham laughed. "Oh, yeah? Look at that—from a scared young kid to a teacher. I like it."

Damian didn't give Max a chance to resolve his growing confusion. He grabbed his arm and shoved him gently but firmly out the room.

"Change and come out when you're ready to leave," he whispered. "I have to take care of this. There's no point in you getting involved with him. Whatever he is here for, it's bound to be beyond the scope of a priest. It's a long story."

Max nodded and entered his room. "If you need me, let me know."

He smiled at the young man and shut the door. Abraham sat at the table, and Damian chose a chair opposite him. The older man held a brass ball from the shelves in his hand and tossed it up and down.

The priest hadn't seen this coming, and he was a little disgruntled by the intrusion. "You think maybe you could've called first, or even waited outside instead of breaking through the door?"

Abraham chuckled arrogantly. "Looks like somebody's lost his sense of humor in his old age."

"Why does everybody keep saying I'm old? I'm not fucking old." He didn't bother to hide his exasperation.

His visitor lifted an eyebrow at his response. "Sounds

like you've been arguing with your demon. I've learned from experience that it's not good to do that. Did you know they have the ability to literally pluck your damn nerves? I'm talking playing them like a harp. It's not the most comfortable thing in the world."

Damian leaned forward, grabbed the ball in midair, and set it down hard on the table. "It's also not good to break into someone's house after not seeing them or speaking to them for over a decade, Abraham. Not to mention that the last time I saw you, you and your girlfriend were being chased down the main strip of Vegas by a pack of pissed-off demons. Those same demons stopped and threw a bus full of old people three blocks in an attempt to hit you. You cost a lot of lives that day, then, poof, you were gone. No accountability, no thanks for cleaning up your mess, no explanation, nothing."

"It was a wild day, that was for sure. I didn't see that rift coming, and we were swarmed by demons apparently coming out of nowhere. We had to run. Really didn't have any other choice."

The priest looked at him in amazement. "How about the opposite direction, in which you didn't put people's lives at risk? And again, you simply disappeared like a Vegas magician."

Abraham sighed and leaned forward in his chair, his face serious. "I'm sorry about that, but I kind of went off the grid. I needed to. I knew it would just be a matter of time until I walked into the wrong infestation."

Behind them, Max cleared his throat as he opened his bedroom door and stepped out. He walked over to the table and looked at Abraham for a moment before turning to Damian. "I assuming you're not coming with me?"

The priest shook his head. "Not right now. Be careful. I'll throw the pie away later."

The trainee patted him on the shoulder. "Thanks. If you need me, you know how to get hold of me."

Abraham had stood again and was examining the shelves. Max glared at him before he headed out. The older man picked up one of the pictures on the shelf and dusted it with his arm. "Who are these people?"

Damian rubbed his face. "I don't know. The priest before us left all his stuff here."

His visitor glanced up. "He retire?"

He rolled his eyes and pushed himself from the chair. "Yes, but not to Tahiti. More like to the local crematorium."

Abraham grimaced and returned the picture to the shelf. "I have to say, man, I'm really proud of you. You've come a long way. I was shocked when I heard you left the mercs. What was it—like fifteen years or something? Shit, that's dedication, and a really good streak of luck."

Damian simply stared at him. "Or the grace of God."

The man chuckled, looked at a book, and put it back. "You know I don't subscribe to that mumbo-jumbo. I simply don't get the whole 'speaking in tongues and playing with snakes' thing."

The priest scowled in annoyance. "That's not my church. We don't do either of those things. I would think that by now you would know that."

Abraham turned toward him with a thoughtful expression. "Me and you, we really did have some fun times. We kicked some major demon ass, too. It feels like it was about a million years ago, and not even in this lifetime."

Damian moved to rest his hands on the back of the chair facing the fire. "It was the past, and it will stay there. I did some seriously foolish shit back then."

His companion laughed and pointed a bony finger at him. "You remember the time with that old lady and her oxygen tank? *Boom*—"

The priest raised his hand to cut him off. "Abraham! Cut to the chase. What the hell is going on? I know you didn't come here to shoot the shit with me. You've never been that guy."

Abraham bit the inside of his lip in a nervous gesture. "They took my wife, and I don't know if she's still alive."

CHAPTER ELEVEN

The house was silent except for the crackle of the fire and the tap of the man's boots as he paced back and forth in the living room. He clenched his hands behind his back, a grim look in his eyes. Damian had never seen him like that, which was one of the main reasons he continued to listen. In all the years he had known him, he only ever saw him care about killing demons, nothing else. This look told him a completely different story.

Abraham sighed and held his hands behind his head as he walked. The priest could see the outline of his ribs beneath his shirt. He hadn't been taking care of himself, obviously.

He began to explain from the beginning. "It came down to the fact that I'd had enough of the business. It wasn't fun for me anymore, and I craved quiet and normal. I wanted a break, but unfortunately, we can't merely put in for a vacation in our world. I was tired of being on my own even though I still had to explain every decision I made to the government, who got more and more involved."

Damian was surprised. "You hadn't met your wife yet?"

Abraham shook his head. "No, not until about three months later. I had nomaded around, enjoying the beauty that the world had to offer. Downtown in Baton Rouge one night, there was a small incursion. It was in my blood, so I jumped in with the mercs there and started helping. That's when I met Elizabeth. I mean, you met her before. She was gorgeous, feisty, smart, and everything I never knew I wanted in a woman. She softened me."

Damian could see it, but he wasn't about to say anything to the man. Marriage, life, and death…it either softened or hardened you. He had apparently gotten stronger, but from the tired bags under the other man's eyes and the way the shadows crept across his aging face, he could tell that Abraham was on the cusp of letting go. Every man had their breaking point, and his visitor was close to his.

The older man leaned his shoulder against the mantle and stared into the fire. "Me and Elizabeth, we had the same thoughts on life. She was tired of the fight, not because she didn't care but because, like me, she had done her share and had put her life on the line. We both wanted out, and a chance to have a piece of that happy pie the rest of humanity has. I persuaded her to leave it all and come with me. We had only known each other for all of three days at that point, but there was no denying that we were created from the same mold. We were meant for each other."

Damian sighed. "So you simply left."

Abraham smiled to himself. "Yes. We got married and settled down in a small town, bought a house, and lived our lives. We cooked dinner every night, put a Christmas tree up in December, took summer vacations, and did everything else that we hadn't been able to do. It was like our world was exactly what we wanted."

"And your demons?" the priest asked.

Abraham shrugged, his expression guarded. "She didn't have one. She was a volunteer, and I suppressed mine. That's why my body looks so rough. He's not helping me. I learned how to push him down as far as he could possibly go. We wanted a life together, and we didn't want to be forced to share it with anyone else. That's what infection does—it forces you to share your life."

Damian took a sip of the whiskey he had poured before Abraham had started to explain. "Okay, I can understand wanting a real life, and God knows you and Elizabeth did enough in your lifetimes to not let the demons take over. I wonder, though, how you stayed off the grid for so long. No one came looking for you?"

His companion stared at the picture over the fireplace. "No one came looking for me because I was a rogue fighter. People tried to pull Elizabeth back, but when it came down to it, she didn't have to fight, and her merc family wouldn't kill her. After Incursion Day, we finally breathed a deep sigh of relief. It was okay for infected to lead normal lives as long as they didn't affect anyone else. They didn't have to be mercs. Everyone forgot about us, and that was what we wanted—to feel safe and secure in our lives."

The priest shook his head and sighed. "And these

demons who took your wife? You hadn't run into them anywhere along the way?"

Abraham chuckled bitterly. "You know that during my fighting time I pissed off a lot of people and a lot of demons, and I bent more than my share of rules. There's always a possibility it goes back to something I did years ago, but after we left, we never encountered a demon or an incursion. We kept to ourselves. I can't remember a single time since we left Baton Rouge that we even exchanged negative words with someone, much less pissed off a cult of Satan worshippers. The people who took my wife were messengers of a demon. Unfortunately, I have no clue which one."

Damian stood and poured the man a drink. "What happened when they took her?"

He was silent for a moment, and his expression flashed through a variety of emotions. "I went to the market to get something for dinner. It was like any other day. Elizabeth was baking bread—she loves baking. Anyway, I got home, kissed her, and went to put the groceries away. Not even five minutes later, there was a loud bang and infected dressed in robes flooded into the place. I tried to fight, but three of them grabbed me and threw me to the floor. I was too weak by that time. The main guy had punched me hard in the face and kicked me in the stomach."

The old man looked away and rubbed his stomach as if he could remember the pain. "I turned on my side and watched as they dragged Elizabeth kicking and screaming from the house. One demon stood on my back. When she disappeared out the door, it hit me on the back of the head with something hard. All I can remember is everything going black. When I woke up hours later, it was dark, blood from my head had pooled on the floor, and the front door stood wide open. I've seen enough cults in my day to know they were part of a big one."

Damian rubbed his chin thoughtfully and finished his whiskey. "They didn't come when she was alone but waited for you to arrive. And it was only five minutes afterward, which means they planned it that way. It feels damn personal, like whoever orchestrated this wanted you to see it happen. You might be walking into a trap."

Abraham gritted his teeth. "Trap or not, I won't leave my wife there. It's my responsibility to protect her. After I cleaned up, I contacted an old friend who found you for me, and I came straight here."

The priest hadn't realized until that moment how fresh the whole thing was to his companion. He could now see the bruises and the blood caked in his hair. Most likely, he hadn't slept, just left immediately to find him. He took the man's empty glass, refilled it, and handed it to him with a smile. "I think we both need this right about now. I'm sorry that this happened to you. I'm sorry this happened to Elizabeth. The two of you were looking for a sanctuary, and you were robbed of that. It's not fair, whichever way you look at it."

The older man sat and leaned forward with his elbows on his knees and his whiskey clutched in a trembling hand. The priest stared at the floor for a moment, simply waiting until Abraham was ready to continue. The older man glanced at Damian, his expression drawn and tense. "You gotta help me, man. You're the only one I know who can help in this situation. The mercs will want to take over, and they won't view her as precious cargo. She's the only thing I have in this world—the only pure and amazing thing that has ever loved me in return. I can't leave her there to die. I can't give in or give up. I need you, Damian."

He shifted in his seat and sighed. "This is a damn horrible situation. Honestly, it's the first time I've ever heard of a merc targeted in their own home. That makes it a red flag, and a big one."

Abraham nodded. "So you'll help me?"

Damian wanted to say yes, but he had a duty to the church. "It's not as easy as it used to be, Abraham. I'm not a merc anymore. I no longer have freedom of choice, I go where I'm assigned. That's the gist of it. I work directly for the church now, and when I tell you that they watch me, trust me, they *watch* me. They will know if I do something independently. I can, however, put you in touch with people who will be able to help you. I would trust them with my life."

His visitor growled and slammed his glass on the side table. "I don't want help from the damn mercs. They'll systematically turn this into a witch hunt, with my wife considered collateral damage. They can't be trusted, Damian. You know that. You may have a badass one in Katie, but other than that… I'm sorry, buddy, but I don't trust them. It has to be me who goes in there, with someone who knows how important the rescue is."

The priest groaned and threw his hands up. "I honestly don't know how it could be possible."

Abraham shook his head. "Make it possible. I chose you to help me because you're the best. On top of that, I know that if my wife has been infected during this whole hellish nightmare, I can count on you to bring her back. To exorcise her."

Damian winced as a trickle of alarm raced through him. "It's not always that simple, Abraham. It all depends on when she was infected, and how strongly the demon has taken over. Some humans can't be saved from the infestation, so we kill them and let their ashes return to the earth. Even if I am there, it doesn't necessarily mean I'll be able to help her. I don't want you to have high hopes when we're walking into a situation we don't even know the half of."

The man looked at him with despair. "But there *is* hope that you can, right?"

He exhaled a slow, deep breath. "Sure, but I'm not a miracle worker. There are things that are far beyond my control. Some, unfortunately, don't turn out the way we want them to, or even in a way that's fair."

Abraham pointed his finger at him. "Do you remember that night like thirteen years ago in Vegas when we chased those infected showgirls down? They were falling apart at the seams, and we killed all but one. You swore that last one was too far gone, but you tried anyway. I was ready to kill her, but you wouldn't let me. Instead, you brought her back from the brink of death. She survived, even with the damage that the demon had done. It *is* possible, Damian."

Despite his reservations, he couldn't avoid the truth. "It's possible, yes, but it's not probable. We'd be walking into a dangerous situation without backup, and I hate to say this but—"

His companion stood abruptly. "No. Don't even say the words. I know what you think—that she's already dead or done for. She spent years fighting demons without becoming infected, and now she may die from what she avoided for so long. She can't heal herself like you can."

Damian studied his glass, his thoughts rampaging. "I want you to be prepared for the fact that not every situation is the same."

Abraham fell back into the chair and stared desperately at him. "Please, I'm begging you with everything I have. Don't let her die. Don't let us *both* die. You know that if you don't help me, I'll still go on my own. I've fought demons before, and these guys are tough. With the right numbers, they could take me straight down to hell. I need this one last favor from you. You must know that I'd never have come if it wasn't absolutely necessary. If I'd had anywhere else to turn, I would have left you alone. God knows you've done enough for me over the years."

The priest rubbed his chin, hating that he couldn't simply agree. A mission of this magnitude would be almost impossible to keep secret. The church would find out about his involvement, and they wouldn't be happy.

He noticed that his demon was attentive but silent, and he needed her input. *What do you think, Ravi? Should I do this?*

She sniffed her disapproval. *I, of course, am not too excited about the idea of rolling into a cult den with only the two of you. We don't have the manpower or the weapons to make this situation safe. At the same time, though, I can't help but wonder who this large demon is who has targeted your friend.*

Damian scoffed. *Knowing him it could be anyone, but for some reason, I trust him when he says he hasn't been in any squabbles lately.*

Ravi considered it for a second. *I can still smell the demon on Abraham. It's not any scent I've encountered before, even in hell. I don't know what to make of it, really. I wasn't aware that they were hiding demons down there that none of us knew about. Still, I can't say I'm surprised.*

He waited for her to continue.

Her sigh sounded disappointed. *The truth is, we need to know who these demons are, what the cult is, and where it's all going. Fighting with Abraham might ease your conscience, and at the same time give you some real insight into what is happening out there. It might be in your best interests to do this for him. Plus, I can tell he used to be a warrior, and that's not a bad thing to have in your Rolodex. It might be worth the blood.*

CHAPTER TWELVE

Damian put up his hands as Abraham continued his entreaty. "Stop. You have to stop begging me like this. You have been in my life for nearly fifteen years, and I can't say that all of it was a positive experience. Nonetheless, I consider those I fight with family, which means that your family is my family. I won't let this happen to your wife without doing everything I can to help."

"Thank you." The man's eyes went wide with relief.

The priest shook his head. "This is the last time, though. I take my vow to the church very seriously. I cannot break that every time something bad happens. You, better than anyone, should know that the world is kind of hell on Earth right now. I have to focus on my calling after this rescue attempt. Also, I need you to grasp the truth that I might not be able to help her if she has become infected. You can't lose it on me in the middle of a battle."

Abraham nodded. "I understand. The odds aren't

perfect. I get it, but I *know* that we can make this work. I have to try. I can't leave her there."

"I applaud you for thinking about someone besides yourself. It's refreshing to see that."

His companion clapped his hands decisively. "Let's get going, then. I'm sure we can track them down pretty fast."

Damian snorted but smiled to take the sting out of it. "Hold up. I've learned a few things over the years that have kept me alive longer than most other mercenaries. One of those is to never rush into a situation. The right preparation can mean the difference between life and death. When emotions are high, you run blind, and we both know how tricky demons can be. From the sound of it, the cult members aren't only strong, but smart, too. For a demon-infested person on the wrong side, that can be very dangerous."

He tapped his fingers on his lips as he thought out loud. "I have to make a couple of phone calls. I know people with access to information and weapons, so we should be able to go in as prepared as we can be for this situation."

Abraham cleared his throat. "The longer we wait, the more likely it will be that she is infected or dead."

"I know this is important to you, which is why you need to think before you leap." The priest put his hand on the man's shoulder. "You don't want to be the reason she dies when we run in with guns blazing and nothing to back it up. You came to me because this is what I do, and now I need you to trust me."

Abraham agreed, although his face revealed his reluctance. "I know you won't steer me wrong, brother."

"Hey, I'm back," Max yelled from the hallway.

They turned in their seats as he entered the room. Giving the visitor only a brief glance, he held up the two bags in his hands. "I bought a bunch of different coffees from around the world. We could have a taste test to see which ones we liked the best."

Abraham smirked. "Your demon likes coffee? Mine liked chocolate. It was a pain in the ass, and I constantly had to hit the gym. Coffee seems like a pretty good one."

Damian smiled, stood, and walked to Max, who waited expectantly. "We have something to work on, and as much as I want to participate in a coffee binge, it will have to wait. I won't have time for it for a few days. I would have told you before you left, but things turned out different than I expected."

The older man sauntered to the bookshelf and tried not to listen to the conversation even though he found it absolutely hilarious. At the same time, he knew how important it was for the Damned to have a piece of regular life. That was what he was now fighting for, after all.

Max's lip popped instantly into a pout. "That fracking sucks."

Abraham turned quickly. "Fracking?"

Damian shook his head at him. "Just don't."

Max was incredibly disappointed, and his demon was livid. *Are you fucking serious? I finally get all the coffee I can drink, and this clown and his sideshow freak over there want to postpone it. No. Hell, no.*

The trainee sighed. *We should include him on this. I'll make some of them without him, though, to curb that craving. It's seeping over into me. I feel like a pregnant woman craving pickles and ice cream.*

That's disgusting. Humans are disgusting, doing all kinds of weird shit as they incubate other humans inside their bodies. Weird. God is totally fucking weird.

Damian pulled him aside. "I'm sending you on a trip. You leave tomorrow morning. I'll give you my card, and you can book yourself a flight immediately. I want you to pack for it right away. Trust me, you'll enjoy this, and I bet you get to try even more coffee."

Astaroth growled. *Now he is shooing us out like a child.*

Max was irritated, but not as badly as his demon. *For whatever reason he wants us to leave, but I trust his judgment.*

You would.

He glanced at the other two men. "Where am I going?"

His mentor smiled. "You're going to Blanchland here in England to study historical sites there that have been linked to heavy demon activity through history."

Abraham chuckled, drawing their attention. "I went there once. It was one hell of a time. Let's just say it involved a demon chase and a girl named 'Sweet Tits.'"

Max winced and glared at the visitor, then grabbed Damian by the arm and led him into the other room. After a quick glance to make sure the man hadn't followed, he lowered his voice. "Do you need help with anything? Whatever is going on here, something doesn't feel right. I don't feel comfortable about leaving you right now. You don't have to tell me the details, but if you need more hands, let me know. I won't say a word to the Wise Men. They don't need to know everything."

Damian was impressed with Max's willingness to help. "I really appreciate the camaraderie; it speaks volumes for how far you've come. Unfortunately, I think this one is a little over your head, and I can't risk losing you in a battle that isn't church-sanctioned. I can't take the chance of losing you ever, actually, but at least this way you get a vacation until I get him out of my hair. We also have the opportunity to save a life. Go to Blanchland, do your happy tourist thing, and when you get back, things will be back to normal. I promise."

The young man's expression remained wary. "Are you sure? If this is something the church doesn't think I can handle, I want to know. They can't put me in some dangerous situations and pull me from others."

His mentor shook his head. "No, it's not church-sanctioned. It's personal. I hope to get it over with as quickly as possible, but you know me—I gotta be prepared. Having you away from here and involved in something that's not dangerous will relieve some of my stress. I have to make sure you're safe."

"All right—not that I have very much choice in the matter. I know that when you make up your mind about something, there's no changing it." Max shrugged, the gesture resigned rather than enthusiastic.

Damian chuckled. "No, I suppose not."

"What will I be studying while I'm there? Is there a book of demon involvement in historical events I should look for in the library?"

The priest laughed and gestured for Max to follow him into the library. He moved from shelf to shelf and pulled down different historical references and some journals. As he piled them into the trainee's arms, he grinned. "That should do it. Brush up on everything, and take as many as you can with you. I'll make a call and set you up with one of my buddies—a priest—from back in the day. He'll give you some really good information on demon activity throughout history. This guy knows everything about these sites, and more. He can probably provide a better background on the stuff I told you in Rome, too."

Max stared at the stack in bemusement. "I'll have to check an extra bag, and it'll weigh like a hundred pounds."

His mentor pulled his card from his pocket and put it on top. "Do whatever you need to."

The young man sighed and walked from the library to his room. Damian stood in the doorway of the living room until he was out of earshot. Abraham hadn't heard him return, and simply stood there and stared into the fire. Making the decision to help had been hard, but seeing how lost the man looked, he really couldn't have refused. He had a gut feeling, though, that things wouldn't work out quite as he wanted them to. That seemed to be the story of the rogue fighter's life, unfortunately—always behind the curve and always on the receiving end when the shit hit the proverbial impeller.

The older man pulled himself from his haze and sat once more. "So, what is the first thing we need to do? I don't want to waste any time. The longer we dilly-dally here, the more danger she's in. I know I don't have to tell you that, but I can't help it."

Damian understood the sentiment and responded patiently, "She's your wife. I understand your anxiety. I promise we'll work as fast as possible. The first thing we need to do is peg this group down. We need to make sure that we have every piece of information we can find on them. I want to know an estimated number, are they national or international, and what demon they worship. Hell, I want to know what they fucking brush their teeth with. I don't want to underestimate my opponent."

Abraham dug through his pocket and pulled out a wrinkled piece of paper. "I knew I would need some information to pass along, so I did some reconnaissance on my own before I came here. The place they took Elizabeth to is only about three hours from here. I called an old contact of mine, and he responded before I arrived. It's a schoolhouse. I wrote the address here."

He slid the paper across to Damian, who was surprised he had done anything at all. The rogue fighter had always been the kind of guy who flew by the seat of his pants. The priest could only assume that his love for his wife had slowed him down enough to at least try to think about the details. He nodded his head. "This is good, really good. Creepy that it's in a schoolhouse, but hey, they thrive on creepy."

Abraham cracked a smile. "That they do. Anyway, that's where they're keeping her, and we need to eventually end up there. Apparently, it's abandoned and hasn't been maintained since it closed down years ago. It's off the beaten track, and there is enough space that the cult can monitor everything going on there. It sounds like a dangerous place, but with the right weapons, I think we can pull it off."

Damian folded the paper and pulled his phone from his pocket. He didn't want to waste another second. They had too much to do, and the clock was ticking. Focused, he flipped through the numbers, but before he could dial, his companion put his hand up. "Who are you calling? I thought this would stay between us. I don't trust other people to keep their mouths shut, and the last thing I need is to walk into a trap because someone blew our cover. It has to be top secret."

The priest put the phone down for a second and stared seriously at him. "I know you're scared, and possibly even paranoid right now. Still, if you want me to be part of this mission, you have to trust me. One thing I'm adamant I will never do again is to walk blindly into a building. To avoid that, I need maps, surveillance, and a whole slew of other things that I don't have here on my shelves. Take a deep breath. I've never steered you wrong before."

Abraham leaned back nervously, and Damian could tell he needed a little more reassurance. "You remember that trip to Southern California?"

The man smirked. "Yeah, the one where we freaked all those people out so we could use the pool ourselves?"

He laughed. "Yes. What I remember even more is the battle we charged into without any knowledge of what was happening. That was one of the worst beatings I've ever endured. We both ended up in the hospital. You were stabbed in the kidney by a demon, and I had four broken ribs, a concussion, and a gash that ran the length of my spine. It wasn't something I even saw coming. I won't go through that again. You know I lost a lot of men with the mercs. They were brave and beautiful souls who will never return."

The rogue fighter knew all this, but it didn't allay his reservations. "I'm afraid to involve other people, not only because of trust issues but for safety. If others are there, I'll feel the need to protect them instead of focusing on what has to be done. Besides, I remember your contacts. They're always hella shifty, and you don't exactly brag about them in public."

Damian pursed his lips. "I was a baby then. I wanted the movie-screen battle scene. Things are definitely different now. I have some really good resources, and to do this effectively, I think it needs to be carefully planned. I trust these people with my life. I use everything they send me, and most of the time they're involved in my battles, even if it's only from behind the scenes. I sent Max away because he's too inexperienced, which means I need to compensate for his loss by including as much reconnaissance as possible."

CHAPTER THIRTEEN

Damian grunted as he backed into the front door and opened it. He balanced the large paper bag on his knee and tossed his keys on the stand by the door. Turning, he kicked the door shut behind him and walked into the living room. Awkwardly, he set the package on the table near the fire and stood to ease his back with a satisfying crack. He hadn't realized how out of shape he had gotten and made a mental note to schedule workouts in the coming days. With all the fighting, his training regimen had all but lapsed, but after the day he'd had, he looked forward to doing nothing but relaxing.

He walked into the kitchen and drank a tall glass of water while he leaned against the counter and looked around. Max had apparently cleaned while he was gone, which he was thankful for. No matter how neat and tidy he was with his appearance, he tended to be messy in the kitchen, and most of the time, he didn't even cook. He wasn't sure how it always turned out looking like he was a master chef who disdained dishwashing.

The priest finished his water and returned to the main area. He paused in the dining room and looked at the stack of notes he had written with Abraham. It would be a huge fight, he could feel it, and he wasn't entirely sure the older man was up to it. He had offered him a room at the house, but Abraham had declined and booked a room in a London hotel for some "quiet time." Damian knew what that meant. He planned to get wasted and wallow in self-pity for a while. He didn't like it, but he had given up babysitting the rogue fighter a long time ago.

The rest of the house was eerily silent except for the crackling fire. Max had gone to bed already, having packed his things and booked his flight. He couldn't tell if the trainee was upset about the whole thing or not, but it had to be done. Part of being a mentor to the kid was to keep him safe, and he didn't intend to drag him into one of Abraham's mishaps, no matter how badly he felt for Elizabeth. He knew there had to be more to the story, even if Abraham didn't know what it was.

Damian could still remember Elizabeth, even though he had only fought with her a handful of times. He remembered hearing about her leaving the team in Louisiana, but he'd never thought to ask whether she returned. Life had been crazy back then, with demons calls every other day. Other people going M.I.A. had been the least of his worries at that point.

He drew a deep breath and caught the lingering aroma of Max's coffee experience. It was strong in the air, but he didn't mind. It made him think back to when he lived at the barracks with the mercenary teams. Before Katie, the place had smelled like stale coffee all the time, but after she came, a fresh pot was always ready. She didn't even drink much coffee back then. Her beverage of choice had been a cup of tea, even at the bar. But she made sure that her family was taken care of, and coffee was their elixir of life.

It made him crave a hot cup, but he had other things on his mind. There were much better drinks available, and he planned to have a little fun that night in the process. He rarely ever took time for himself, so he didn't feel guilty about it in the least.

Damian wandered to the liquor cabinet, opened it, and selected several whiskey glasses. He couldn't help but wonder why a home predominantly used to house priests would have such an extensive liquor cabinet, but he shrugged and decided it was merely a happy accident. There wasn't anything stocked there that he wanted, mostly sherry and a couple of bottles of expensive port. It was exactly the kind of thing that he could see old, over-weight priests sitting around drinking when they plotted something nefarious for the church. There were definitely enough of that kind of priests.

He dusted the glasses and could sense Ravi's attention quickening. He knew she would be excited, but he tried to wait to tell her until after he'd formulated his plan of attack.

She yawned. *Whatcha doing with those glasses, Pops?*

The priest smirked. *You'll see. Just be patient.*

If you haven't noticed, I'm a demon. Patience isn't something that was instilled in us when we were created or turned into demons. Nonetheless, carry on.

Damian laughed as he walked back into the living room to the shopping bag. He put the glasses on the table and pulled six different bottles of liquor from it and set them in a row. Ravi took a second to look everything over and sniffed each one. *You are my goddamn hero, Pops. I'm so fucking stoked. I seriously thought you would never make good on your promise.*

He shook his head. *You didn't give me any time. Seriously. You ask for something, and you want it right then. For someone centuries old, I figured you would have learned how to wait.*

I know you love me, despite the fact that you just put an age on me. I'll ignore that for now. I knew it, though. I knew it. Yes, sir, I knew it. Sometimes, I lose faith in you, Pops. I do. But in the end, you never cease to amaze me.

Damian laughed, feeling like he had given her a second chance at life or something. It was only scotch. He decided that if he were stuck inside someone else, constantly working on them, he would get excited over something like that too. *You have to rev up my tolerance, though. I really don't want to have a hangover tomorrow. I also don't want to end up stumbling into Rose's arms in the middle of the night. She might feed me, and then all hell would break loose.*

Ravi sneered. *I'll take that bitch out. Seriously. I'll take her down to hell and contort her body into a damn apple tree, and when she is full of apples, I'll fucking bake her. Baked Rose. Lucifer would love it.*

The priest's eyes went big. *Calm down there, Hannibal. I think I will be fine. You don't need to go killing old ladies for me.*

Not for you, for the pie.

He chuckled at her weird but honest humor. *Sometimes, I'm really happy to have someone in my head to make me laugh.*

Talking to myself started to get weird after a while. Although I do have God, He rarely ever says anything back.

The demon smirked. *I have a secret for you. Anyone who says they have heard the voice of God is a liar. That was one of the rules He put on himself when He created you. He would never talk to humans. He would always send angels or prophets to do it. He put his magic on it, and it can't be undone, even by Him. Pretty impressive, in my opinion.*

That's pretty neat.

She sighed. *Mhmm. Okay, so what do we got here?*

Damian rubbed his hands together. *First, we have Monkey Shoulder Blended Scotch. It's a blend of Speyside single malt scotchs with a fruity aroma infused with mellow vanilla. It is aged in former bourbon casks, which is where the vanilla comes from.*

Mmm, that sounds freaking delicious. And there are monkeys on the bottle. That's seriously amazing. It signifies to me that these gents have some taste.

The priest raised an eyebrow. *Okay... Next is the Hudson Baby Bourbon. It's made by the Tuthilltown distillery in Hudson, New York, which has been open since the time of Prohibition. It has hints of charred American oak barrels and is slightly sweet with a roasted corn flavor.*

Ravi shivered. *Prohibition...that was a nasty time in America. You fools find something that makes most of you nicer, and you take it away. I think the rulers of this place want the people to be grumpy and unhappy. Or they really like to torture themselves. Though I have to admit, the men who came up with the rule were probably the worst when it came to smuggling it in.*

Damian shook his head. *That didn't last long. Now, the next one I got is ten-year-old Whistle Pig Rye. It is a hundred-*

proof one hundred percent rye whiskey. It has warm wooden notes with hints of vanilla, caramel, dried orange peel, cinnamon, allspice, and clove.

She gagged. *Sounds like bottling autumn and calling it a whiskey. But a hundred-proof makes me think it'll be one badass whiskey.*

There are also hints of creamy flavors, leaving notes of dark chocolate too. Then there is the Glendronach eighteen-year-old Sherry Cask. It's a single malt scotch with characteristics of ginger, orange, cherry walnut, dark chocolate, and...Christmas cake.

How do you make something taste like Christmas cake? The demon laughed loudly. *And hold up. What the hell does Christmas cake actually taste like? I'm really confused here.*

The priest wasn't sure either. *I guess we'll find out. The last two I got are the same company, Highland Park, but I got the ICE edition and the Loki. There are only 3915 bottles of the ICE floating around, and I got one. It was matured in ex-bourbon casks.*

And it comes in that nifty holder. How old is it?

Damian looked at the label. *Seventeen years old. The Loki has a hint of orange and lemon. It apparently smells like gingerbread and has water, licorice, and aromatic smoke scents. I'm not really sure what aromatic smoke is.*

Ravi snickered to herself. *You humans create a lot of aromatic smoke. Most of the time, it makes people want to vomit all over themselves.*

That's disgusting. If we'll be tasting scotch and whiskey—some upward of six hundred dollars a bottle—you're not allowed to comment about bodily functions. It makes me want to simply go to bed. Don't disrespect these like that.

She agreed hastily. *You're right. I should bow to the altar of the bottles, but instead, I'm being obnoxious. Straight-faced the rest of the time. Promise.*

Damian was surprised at how well that had worked. Ravi had to be dying to try the different bottles if she actually apologized and blew off things like that. He wouldn't complain, though. It was pleasant to have an amicable relationship. Back in the day, they would never have been able to sit down for something like this, so they had both come a really long way and tried to meet somewhere in the middle.

He grabbed the Monkey Shoulder and poured a splash in the glass. With elaborate care, he swished it around and inhaled the aroma of the alcohol. He took a sip and smacked his lips. Ravi went silent as she tasted the scotch. When she was done, she cheered in his head. *That one was awesome. It was smooth and vanilla-ish, but still held the traditional scotch flavor. I like it.*

The priest concurred, and began tasting one after the other. He poured another splash of the ones they both liked the most. The demon did her best to absorb the liquor and speed up his metabolism, but she wasn't a pro at it. Despite her efforts, after two hours he was drunk, and she could feel a slight buzz herself. She made a smacking sound in his ear. *So far, I would have to say the Loki is my favorite.*

Damian was surprised. *Really? I would have taken your demon self for a lover of the burnt flavors of the Tuthilltown. You know, something like home.*

Ravi snorted drunkenly. *You kill me, Pops. No, I mean it.*

You kill me, keeping me bottled up in here. I like the bitter orange and lemon flavors of the Loki.

He stood, walked jerkily to the dining room, and grabbed his fallen angel book off the table. Back in the living room, he sat cross-legged on the floor and opened it. *I think it's time for the educational portion of the evening. What do you think?*

OK, as long as you don't start to hiccup. I can't stand that.

The priest was too busy flipping sloppily through the pages of the book to react. Finally, he simply tossed it on the floor, leaned back on his hands, and stretched his legs out in front of him. *Tell me some fallen angel lore. I like to hear my people's insane legends.*

She giggled. *Oh, goodie. This is my favorite. Well, let's see, stupid human angel lore. Irish folklore is a good place to start. They believed that there were fairies, which were actually angels fallen from heaven. They put tiny houses out for them.*

Like that video we watched where that woman bakes the tiny cake for the hamster. Damian chuckled, the image vivid in his mind.

Ravi hated that video. *Ugh, don't remind me. Then there is the folklore about God and Azazel and his journey on Earth. Apparently, he was one of the leaders of the two hundred angels, but he lusted after some human booty. God punished him by casting him down to Earth—which was dumb, really, 'cause that's where all the booty was. Anyway, he recruited giants or something to pillage and ended up becoming a demon djinn. We've all heard the story, but no one knows if it's true.*

Damian swayed as he listened to her. *Wasn't there some lore about giants?*

Oh, yeah. That one's true, though. They said that the giants were the guardians of the fallen angels' children—the ones who came down and got...it...on. They ended up killing the children and were cast into hell. Those are the big motherfuckers you have to deal with all the time. They are the rape-y giants from early on.

He wrinkled his nose and laid back on the rug, yawning. *Great. Not only do we have to fight demons, but we have to fight rape-y ones. I'll be sure to remember that. I know Pandora has a thing for lopping dicks off whenever she can.*

Yep, she was like that in hell too. No dicks were safe when she was angry. Walk into a room, and whoops, tripped over a stump of cock on the floor. Gotta tread carefully.

That makes me want to puke. Damian grimaced.

Ravi groaned. *No, I think that's the Whistle Pig.*

CHAPTER FOURTEEN

Maps stepped over a pile of papers and picked up one of her books. She glanced at Abraham, who stared at her maps, and narrowed her eyes. For some reason, she couldn't help but give him side glances. She dusted the book off and continued her exploration, looking for anything that could help her. It was incredibly hard to do, though, with the rogue fighter creeping around.

She took an old compass from his hand and replaced it on the shelf. It was the fourth time she'd had to rescue something. He couldn't seem to get it through his head that her apartment wasn't a museum. She had gone to great and sometimes dangerous lengths to acquire many of the things she had. They paid her bills, but they also held secrets that she didn't want someone like him getting hold of. She tried to be nice, but Damian could see the frustration on her face.

He walked over and tapped the man on the shoulder. "Look but don't touch."

Abraham rolled his eyes. "Yes, Mother. This is an impressive collection of things, though. I have to say, she has a talent for finding the unusual. I always throw stuff away, and a year later wish I had kept it. Kind of makes me want to scream."

The priest chuckled and winced at the slight pounding in his temples from the hangover that Ravi had tried desperately to remove. "That's why we love Maps. She is on top of it and has all the stuff we thought we would never want but end up needing. Honestly, she can find anything, anywhere, any time. She is a mastermind when it comes to this kind of thing."

He winked at her as she piled stuff on her desk. She nodded in thanks and began typing on her computer. "Give me the address."

Damian pulled the paper from his pocket and began to walk forward, but Abraham stopped him. "You're sure this is the right thing to do? You can trust her, right?"

Maps grumped and kept her gaze fixed on her keys. Damian patted him on the shoulder. "I trust her with my biggest secrets."

He placed the paper beside her. She smiled at him and glared up at his companion. "Is that all the information you have?"

The rogue fighter pulled another scrap of paper from his pocket and set it beside the first. It was a newspaper clipping of a missing student from a local college. "That's one of the boys who was there when they attacked. He's the one who hit me in the head with something and knocked me the fuck out."

She nodded and looked at the paper. It would definitely

be helpful, although she hated that it came from him. He was shifty, like so many other clients she had to work with on a daily basis. She tried desperately not to let that bother her, though. She had a job to do, and she wanted to do it for Damian. She trusted him and his judgment when it came to the people around him. Whoever that guy was, she figured they had a past, especially since Damian was taking on an incredibly dangerous job just to help the man.

She typed faster on the computer and glanced up from time to time to monitor Abraham. He had settled and now kept his hands in his pockets. At least he was no longer touching things, even though she knew he surreptitiously read some of the documents on top of the piles. "You guys can wander around or have a seat. It'll take me a few minutes to get all this done. But please don't touch anything. I have everything organized in a system."

The older man looked at the stacks and piles. "I can see that. Very nice."

Damian accompanied him along the wall, and they studied the pictures hanging there. The display varied from photos of famous murderers, maps of ancient historical sites, and several pictures of the same woman and man. The priest wondered if they were Maps' parents, but decided that was a conversation for another day since Abraham was with them.

The rogue fighter glanced at her and raised his eyebrows. "You always manage to have fucking hot chicks as your friends. First, that girl who used to be on your team...Melissa. Then Katie? Whoa, fucking *steaming* hot. And now this one. Granted, she's a bit strange, but I can dig the goth thing."

The priest kept his eyes trained on the pictures, knowing his companion was trying to get a rise out of him. He tended to do that when he was bored. "Do I need to remind you that I am a man of the cloth? You know, gave my life to God, made a vow of celibacy? These women are all strong and independent people whom I greatly respect."

Abraham chuckled. "Oh, yeah, I'm sure. But does that vow of celibacy mean you no longer have a libido?"

"No, it means I'm a human being who can control myself. I know that is foreign to you and all, but it does exist."

His companion scowled. "Hey, I've been with Elizabeth for years, and I have never cheated on her once—and let me tell you, I had the chance to. But I was faithful, so yes, I know what control is, asshole."

"Good for you. It's a lot better than the way you used to be. You had a different girl every night."

"I was kind of a suave guy back then, wasn't I?" He smiled and tilted his head back.

Damian somehow managed to keep a straight face. "No, girls like bad boys. I can't say your choice was based on their brains."

Abraham grinned. "Hey, I wasn't trying to get their brains into my bedroom. I also didn't plan on ever meeting anyone I wanted to be around for more than a few hours, and talking really wasn't involved."

"Oh? How did Elizabeth get so lucky?"

The older man elbowed him. "I tried at first, but she wouldn't have it. Next thing I knew, I was immersed in our conversation. I don't know…she changed me, I think. At least, she changed me for her. Doesn't mean I don't still look when I see a beautiful woman. I appreciate the female body. I appreciate the delicacy of their features and the way they're strong but soft."

Damian looked at him with distaste. "Yeah, I'm sure that's exactly what runs through your mind when you look at a woman. 'Oh, she has such delicate features.'"

His smirk was telling. "Something like that. Man, I would love to get inside your head and know what you really think about. I want to know how many times you have a normal-man moment when you walk past a beautiful woman."

Ravi yawned. *He should know it's not very often. It's not very exciting up here. Don't get me wrong, I'm not complaining. I would hate to hear about tits and ass all day. That would definitely put a damper on our demon-to-human relationship. Your friend is kind of an ass.*

He's got a good heart in there...somewhere.

"Okay, so there isn't a ton of information about this cult on the surface," Maps said as she approached with a single sheet of paper.

Damian glanced at Abraham and gave him a stern look to remind him to behave. "What did you find out?"

She seemed disappointed. "Just that they originated in Los Angeles, but the cult itself goes back decades. They have chapters here and there but are relatively small right now. Surprise, surprise, there are wars among the cults, and they were extensively thinned out during the sixties."

"That's it?" The older man sighed.

Maps' head snapped up, and Abraham cringed visibly at her glare. "For now. You came with an impossible task, and I made something of it. Don't get all high and mighty."

Damian put up his hands before his companion could say anything. "Thank you. That's a good start."

She took a deep breath and turned her back on Abraham, who grinned at her. "I'll continue to look for information, and as soon as I find out more, I'll contact you. These guys may be thin on the ground, but from what I can see they're still dangerous. Very organized. They also maintain strict secrecy. Most sites that previously had information no longer provide anything. Even on the dark web, sites have been destroyed."

The rogue fighter looked down at his fingernails. "Maybe you aren't as good as Damian says."

Maps growled at him. "Obviously, if you were as good as you say you are, you wouldn't be standing in my place right now asking for *my* help."

Damian put his hand up. "Okay, kids, let's try to calm this down. Thank you again, Maps. Give me a call when you have anything else." Damian started to turn but stopped abruptly. "Oh, and you know that book you got me before?"

She thought about it for a second. "Yeah, yeah. The one about…yeah."

"I get it. You want privacy." Abraham rolled his eyes.

He headed for the door. The priest lowered his voice and leaned in. "I'd really like to find out more about the fallen angels. Things that aren't available to the public. If you can find any of that, it would be really awesome, although I imagine it might be difficult. There's no rush on it. Take your time, but I would love to see it."

Maps gave him a thumbs-up. "Sure, no problem. I actually have a contact who handles stuff like that. I'll see what he can dredge up for me. Folklore is so crazy, and it's all over the place. It's hard to recognize what is or isn't true."

"I know. Luckily, my demon knows a fair amount about it and can usually spot the bullshit from the beginning. She just doesn't know enough to satisfy my curiosity, I suppose."

She shot him an inquiring look. "May I ask why you want to know?"

Damian shrugged. "When I met Katie and Pandora, my interest was kindled. Then I found out what I suspected all along—that Pandora was a fallen angel—and it grew from there. I guess I'm trying to understand her a little better and figure out some of their secrets. They seem relevant enough in this time period with the war and everything."

"I agree."

He gave her a hug. "I'll talk to you soon. Let me get this guy out of here before you two end up in a dogfight."

The priest found Abraham peering into a cabinet, grabbed his arm, and dragged him to the door. The older man looked at Maps and waved. She gave him a tight-lipped smile and flipped him her middle finger. He gasped as they walked out the door. "Your friend isn't very nice. I like it."

Damian was done with that conversation. "Come on, asswipe. Let's grab some food."

They headed to one of the pubs and ordered food and beers. The priest didn't drink beer often, but after last night he didn't really feel like anything harder. As they ate, they talked about old times and how much Abraham missed it sometimes. He shared his inner thoughts, something he hadn't done before. "When you're in the thick of it, you just want out. Then, when you're chilling, relaxing at your house with nothing to do, you start thinking about the fight. You almost crave the adrenaline. I bet you fight ten times harder now because you don't fight every day."

Damian put a fry in his mouth. "I think you're right, but there isn't an absence of missions either. They're merely different, and I do a lot more exorcisms."

His companion gazed off in the distance. "Elizabeth loved the exorcism part of things. She loved saving lives— or others saving lives, at least. The death part of it got to her a lot more than it did me. She turned hard because of it. I saw that soften a bit over the years, though. I can't believe I put her in this situation. She could die, and it would be all my fault. I should have simply let her go."

Damian put his fingers together and searched for the right response. "You do things for love because you want to be with the person. She loved you just as much. Elizabeth wasn't forced."

He watched Abraham slip further into his depression and realized that words of comfort weren't what he needed. The older man wiped his hands. "I know, but the fact that she could be safe right now, even if she wasn't with me, drives me nuts."

The priest shook his head. "The battles get worse and worse. If she wasn't infected, the two of you running most likely gave her a chance at life. Katie has almost died out there. Elizabeth would have been another face on the wall. The reality is that you need to pull your shit together. We'll do everything we can to get her back. I always told you that your sins would eventually catch up to you. Maybe once we get her back, you can start living a better life. Take this as a sign."

Abraham shook his finger at Damian. "You're fucking right. This is a message from above letting me know that what I did in the past won't slide in the future. When I get her back, I'll make sure to stay on the straight and narrow from then on out. No more killing, no more fighting, and no more filling my body with crap. I want to be a good man, someone God finds comfort in. Or at least fucking give it a shot."

Damian listened to him talk, but he knew it wouldn't be that way. The rogue fighter was a wild guy, and he always had been. It wasn't a conscious choice for him to be a dick; it was merely who he was. As soon as Elizabeth was safe, he would go back to the same old guy he had always been. Hopefully, those emotions would be used to take care of Elizabeth for the rest of her life. There was nothing Damian could do once it was over. Whatever the outcome, it would be what it would be, and Abraham would move forward—he hoped.

CHAPTER FIFTEEN

Damian put his feet up on the patio chair across from him and held the mug of coffee in both hands. He took a sip and closed his eyes as the warm liquid soothed his tired throat. A chill had settled into the air. When he woke up earlier, he had found all the different coffees Max had purchased and sniffed them all until he chose the one he wanted. He did this with one eye barely open, having tossed and turned the night before.

The brew was delicious, probably the best he had ever had. He knew the kid's demon would have something to say about him drinking the coffee, but at that moment, with the cool, crisp air blowing around him, he didn't care all that much. He looked up as Rose creaked her door open, humming to herself, and stepped out with her broom in hand. It was the normal morning routine. She stepped into the world and got things done. Her eyes weren't quite as red that morning as they usually were, but she also hadn't noticed him sitting there.

He cleared his throat so he wouldn't scare her, but she jumped anyway and laughed. "You scared me there. Good morning."

"Morning, Rose. How are you?"

She shivered and looked at the small trees swaying with the breeze inside the courtyard. "It seems the seasons are changing early this year. I don't mind, though. I love the fall, and the winters here in London are simply beautiful."

Damian lifted his cup in salute. "I agree. And it doesn't rain as often in the fall. It's pleasant to sit out here on the patio and sip coffee without a torrential storm coming out of nowhere to wash me away."

She held the broom at her side and tilted her head. "Did young Max have a chance to eat the apple pie yet?"

He was about to speak when Abraham opened the door behind him and ventured out with a cup of coffee and a plate full of pie. Damian hadn't even realized he had arrived yet. The priest raised his eyebrows as the older man sat and took a bite with open enthusiasm. He groaned and chewed. "This is absolutely delicious. Just like my mother made when I was a boy."

Rose giggled, smirking evilly, and her eyes glowed red. She turned and hurried into her house without another word. The rogue fighter paused with the fork still in his mouth, not hiding the fact that he found the woman incredibly strange. "I still don't get why you have a demon living across the way and you haven't done anything about it. You always seemed the type to jump right in and free the old woman from the shackles of her demonhood."

Damian reached slowly across the table and slid the plate of apple pie away. He found the whole thing amusing as hell but tried to stifle a laugh for his companion's sake. Abraham looked at the plate and scowled. "What are you doing?"

"It's funny. She's Damned, but her demon is pretty dumb. He has taken a liking to baking, but his ingredients are focused more toward reducing the mercenary population than providing something for your sweet tooth. We tend not to eat any of her baked goods and usually throw them away. I forgot all about the pie."

The visitor looked at the plate, at the priest, and at the plate again, and rage infused his face as he pushed his chair back and grabbed his stomach. As Damian had hoped, he had successfully connected the dots. He really didn't want to simply state that the old woman was a nuisance and decided it could be a learning experience.

Abraham shook his head. "You let her poison me? Why in fuck's sake would you leave a pie on the counter if it had poison in it? Put a fucking biohazard sign up or something."

The priest chuckled. "You won't die from it. I told you that the demon is an idiot when it comes to its attempts to dispose of the mercenary population. You might want to go inside and use the bedroom upstairs at the end of the hall. It has its own bathroom. I would change my clothes too. Put something comfortable on. I can't imagine you would enjoy the experience in jeans. There should be some clothes in the dresser. I keep my extra stuff in that room. Take whatever you need."

The older man's mouth dropped open. "What am I facing here? Death? Should I go to the hospital?"

Damian waved his hands before he picked up his mug.

"It won't be too bad. You'll have a little diarrhea, and a really bad stomach ache. Possibly some vomiting, but it really depends. I'm not sure which concoction she put in this one."

Abraham's hands balled into fists. "That old bitch. I can teach her a lesson she'll never forget."

He rolled his eyes and stood. "Calm down, grandma beater. She's not really the murderous type, and her demon's not the brightest crayon in the box. I can't do anything about her just yet. The church has protected her since she's been part of the congregation for decades. They are concerned that if I exorcise her, she will die. So, unless she actually tries to murder one of us, we aren't supposed to touch her."

His companion shook his head, crossed his arms, and narrowed his eyes. "If I wasn't relying on you to help me, I would remind you that I'm not part of your church, which makes her fair game. As it is, I have a feeling I don't have much time to debate the issue. Throw the pie away, asshole."

With that, he turned and stomped back into the house. Damian waited until he was inside before he laughed hysterically. He couldn't help it. The situation was so ridiculous. Either Abraham had fried taste buds, or his mother had tried to poison him as a child. The priest couldn't help but assume that the pie tasted a wee bit off considering it had some poisonous chemical in it, so Abraham should have at least suspected a problem.

He glanced at the treat, which had a slight green tint to it. She had pulled out all the stops this time and really tried to stick it to one of them. Damian was glad he hadn't dug into it when he was drunk the other night. He would have had much worse than a hangover to worry about.

Beside him on the table, his phone began to vibrate. He leaned back and picked it up to look at the screen. It was Wally, whom he had waited to hear from for several days. He knew his friend was busy, but the symbols rolled incessantly through his mind. Hopefully, the researcher had figured something out. Otherwise, it would remain a mystery that drove him nuts.

"Wally, it's good to hear from you."

"Damian, so sorry it took me so long. I had to get your email offline from the Vatican. I'm still researching what you sent me, but I already have fathers on the ground to retrieve the artifact. The funny thing is, I couldn't find it in the Pompeii register of artifacts. Either someone screwed the pooch on that one, or someone put it there after the register was compiled."

The priest narrowed his eyes. He hadn't even considered that the mask might not actually be from Pompeii or that someone had placed it there. It was one of the buildings in the rear which was probably checked less often, and it had looked like something placed there by the historical society. Anyone cleaning would have walked right past it without much thought. "Interesting. Well, I knew there was something about it when I saw it. The inscriptions and the symbols were all too familiar. I pulled the other information, and sure enough, they were a match."

Wally seemed excited. "It was definitely a good find. Thank you for that."

Damian looked into his empty coffee mug. "Will you call me as soon as you get the information on it? I'll set up a fax machine in the house to make things easier. You can simply fax the info over. I know you guys aren't up to scratch with all the digital technology."

His friend scoffed. "I'm lucky if there's a mechanical pencil. But yes, as soon as I know, you'll know."

He looked at the house and saw Abraham in the window. "Oh, before you go. I've come upon a situation completely outside the church's parameters. I'll be facing something—or many things—that I'm not completely knowledgeable about, and I wanted your input on it. You have a moment?"

He heard Wally pull out a chair. "Yes, sure. What's going on?"

Damian sighed. "Well, an old friend of mine from a while ago showed up at my house. His wife was taken by some kind of cult that's been around for a few decades, at least. She isn't infected, so time is of the essence if we want to get her back without damage. A contact of mine explained that the cult originated in LA. Apparently, they were extensively thinned out during the sixties when the cults fought among themselves. It will only be the two of us going in on this, and I would like to have better info on who I'll face. I wondered if you've heard anything about a cult like that?"

His friend clicked his tongue a few times, a sure sign of focused thought. "Actually, yeah. I think I know who you might be talking about. There was a group started in LA in the forties. They were a Germanic-type group called the

Descendants of Holle, with Holle meaning hell. They were connected to the Nazis later on, and the group had a mixed population—demons, skinheads, and infected like you. In the sixties, they were targeted by other cults because the others felt they were diminishing the message of 'no human left standing,' since they focused on Jewish people, black people, and minorities in general."

Damian raised an eyebrow. "So, we have a hate group mixed with a demon cult? That sounds nice. Any idea what their strategies are?"

"Well, it's been a long time since I heard anything to indicate they were active," Wally said. "They tend to worship third-rung demons—those who have power and are trying to get ahead but aren't Moloch or Lucifer. These demons feed off their hate, and because these infected are so full of anger, they are easily swayed."

The priest rubbed his chin thoughtfully. "So, they may have a relatively strong demon pulling the strings."

His friend cleared his throat nervously. "I have to tell you, though, they've never been known for random violence. They have a reason for everything they do. If they took this woman, there was a reason behind it, whether it's a connection to her or to your friend. It's most likely a trap."

Damian nodded. "I had already assumed that. My friend hasn't always been the most forthright person, even when killing demons. I assume it's someone after him, and she was the easier target. I made a promise, though, and I always keep my promises. Whatever the situation, I'm going in."

Wally voiced his protest. "They will remember your face, so if you don't kill them, they may target you for interfering. These cults have no set rules or values. They don't care what your promises or intentions are. Be careful out there."

The priest shared his lack of enthusiasm, but he was committed. "I will, thank you."

His friend yawned. "Well, I gotta get going. I will do some more research on these guys to see if I can pull up anything more recent. As soon as I find anything, I'll let you know."

"Appreciate it, and stay safe, Wally," Damian replied and hung up.

He sat there quietly and tapped the phone against his lips as he thought for a minute. His mind made up, he shrugged and dialed Timothy, hoping to get some help. "My favorite priest. What in the world are you doing, sister?"

Damian chuckled. "I miss you guys."

"Aww, we miss you too, Papa Priest. How's London? Is it fabulous? Are there fashion shows everywhere and amazing gay men dressed in British flags?"

The priest shook his head. "No, not really, although I'm certain that if you visited, they would make sure there were."

Timothy snapped his fingers. "They'd better."

He laughed. "What's happening on that side of things?"

His friend sighed. "We're still pulling everything together for the move to the new base. Construction will start soon. Stephanie and Korbin are sifting through their old memories now that they have them back. You know, the normal weird-as-fuck shit that goes on over here. Calvin comes by sometimes, but he is with his lady love in San Diego a lot. Joshua and his backup crew stay in their own little world and just want to get their weapons production back on track. There has been a lot of crazy stuff, and we'll all be glad when it's finally over. How about you?"

Damian groaned. "I'm trying to keep up with this new life. I have an old friend here who needs some help. It's something I'm hesitant to do, but I need to keep my word."

Timothy smacked his lips. "Uh oh, sounds dangerous. You need backup?"

"No, only us. He is adamant about that. I'm collecting all the info I can, though, and will hopefully head out soon. But there's something else that I thought you could help me with."

He perked up. "Oh, yeah? What's that?"

The priest tapped his fingers on the table. "About ten years ago, around April or May, there was an Incursion in an old warehouse that Korbin's Killers went out on. Two judges were there, I believe. I'm pretty sure they were Supreme Court Justices, although they could have been senators. Anyway, we took some artifacts from that incursion. I need to find anything with symbols of cult activity on it. I wondered if you could do a little research and find these artifacts."

Timothy clapped his hands. "Oh, boy, something to occupy my time. It might take me a hot minute since everything is boxed up or in piles."

Damian understood. "Take your time."

"Is there some serious importance to this?" he asked.

The priest shrugged. "I'm not sure, actually. It's a hunch, but I figured it was worth a shot."

Timothy giggled. "My priesty poo, always saving the world."

He tilted his head and grinned. "I gotta try."

CHAPTER SIXTEEN

The next day was quiet. They went about their morning with little purpose except to try to get through it. Abraham had stayed at the house that night but kept mostly to himself. He was quiet and contemplative, something Damian wasn't used to seeing. Around noon, the priest's phone rang. It was Maps.

"Go to the door," she said. "A messenger should walk up right about now."

He raised an eyebrow. "Are you spying on me now too?"

She chuckled. "No, I paid him extra to be there at a specific time. That time is now."

Damian looked up as someone knocked on the door. "Looks like he followed instructions to the letter."

Maps mumbled, "Good, because it cost an arm and a leg."

He opened the door, took a long tube from the messenger, and signed for the item. Once he'd closed the door, he opened the end and withdrew what appeared to be blue-prints. "Are these what I think they are?"

"Sure are. The most up-to-date blueprints of the school. Of course, they don't include damage that might have occurred since it closed down, but it will give you the general layout, as well as the most likely places for these guys to hide."

Damian nodded. "This is awesome. Thanks, Maps."

She sighed. "The bad news is that I haven't been able to find out anything else about this cult. They are seriously hidden, and I wouldn't be surprised if they have a tech who does nothing else but shield them from underground chatter about them."

He wouldn't be surprised either. "I did get a call from my contact in the Catholic Church, Father Wally. He remembered quite a bit about them. Apparently, they were formed in LA in the forties, had German ties, and were self-professed Nazis. They were thinned out because they weren't focused on killing everyone."

Maps snorted. "Just the Jews and the minorities. Oh, poor things."

Damian laughed. "Yeah, I don't have a lot of sympathy for them. They are comprised of demons, infected, and skinheads. They worship third-level demons, and apparently always have a reason for everything they do. Definitely not what I imagined I'd face, but they seem more down to earth than most of the cults. I assume Abraham did something to one of their people long ago. I don't know for sure, though. I guess we'll find out later. Or maybe never. It depends, I suppose. My main focus is to get in and rescue Elizabeth, hopefully all in one human piece."

She tried to sound comforting. "Right, well, good luck to her. I know she must be terrified out of her mind. If you guys need anything else from me, let me know. I'll keep the search open, and if I see any last-minute stuff, I'll send it to you."

"Thanks, Maps. I'll get the money to you ASAP." Damian hung up.

Abraham walked nonchalantly into the room as he stuffed the last of a donut into his mouth. He glanced at the rolled-up blueprint on the table. "Is that for us?"

Damian unrolled the sheet and stood to study it. "Sure is. It's the full blueprint of the place where they are holding your wife."

The older man dusted the powdered sugar from his hands and hurried to join him. "Excellent. Let's get down to business."

The priest glanced at him for a moment, nodded, and grabbed a tablet of paper. "So, we want to plan the best route for entry. Looking at this for the first time, two places jump out at me— the back entrance and this side entrance. The side leads you into where the offices are and the waiting area for the school. The back enters into the hallway to the gym and the janitorial areas."

Abraham tapped his finger on the side door. "I think this is where we should go in. I want to have space if there are tons of demons waiting for us. If we go into these halls not knowing what is stacked or blocking the area, we could put ourselves in a corner."

Damian rubbed his chin and focused hard. "I think you might be right. If we take the side entrance, it leads through into what looks like a lobby, a stairwell, and finally, a door that opens into the gym. We can access virtually any point in the place and won't have to walk through the main entrance with our balls out."

His companion pointed to the gym. "If they are set up in the school, this will most likely be their main area, although we can't be sure if they will hold Elizabeth there or in one of the classrooms upstairs. We'll have to figure that out once we get into the building and tackle some of the offensive reactions from the cult."

He looked at him, impressed. "I didn't think you had the ability to look ahead at things like this."

Abraham shrugged. "When you said you wanted to be prepared, I changed my mindset. I can't roll in with my wang out and shoot the place up like I want to. I need your help, so I do it your way, which means mental preparation is key."

Damian nodded astutely. "Precisely. And this looks like a good deal. If all else fails, there is an emergency exit at the rear of the gym, but I want to try to stay away from that. Walking into the gym almost ensures that we will be attacked hard."

His companion chuckled. "The looks on their faces will be priceless, though. We'll need some weapons. Can your girl Maps get us what we need?"

He thought about it for a second and shook his head as he gestured toward the garage. "I don't think we'll need that. Come with me."

The priest led Abraham through the house and into the garage. He removed the key from around his neck and inserted it into the large lock on the metal cabinet in the corner, then slid it to the side and opened both doors to display the weapons he had on hand. Handguns rested on the lower shelf, a crossbow to the right, several automatic weapons up front, and a plethora of knives and swords hung on the doors. In small compartments in the middle were hand grenades, multiple boxes of bullets, and tactical gear.

The man's mouth dropped open, and he stepped forward to pull a Beretta pistol from the side. "Wow, I did not expect this. I mean, you're a priest with an arsenal like RoboCop, for fuck's sake. Do they even allow you to have this shit?'"

Damian winced. "To have it? Yes. To use it? No. Then again, this is our battle, so the church won't be involved. Go ahead and pick out what you want and set it on the tables over there."

They went through the arsenal and chose their weapons carefully. This was the only part of the ordeal that Damian didn't mind. It reminded him of working with the mercs and gearing up before a battle. When they were done, he grabbed two duffel bags and threw one to the other man. "Go ahead and load up. We might as well be prepared for this. At this point, we have all the information we'll get, I think, so we'd better not wait any longer. We'll leave when the sun starts to go down and get there at the perfect time."

Abraham's expression became almost giddy. The adrenaline hit him like a freight train. "*That's* what I'm talking about. My girl has waited *too* long for me to come to rescue her."

They loaded everything into the SUV and added extra weapons and ammo in case they needed them, not that

Damian imagined they would be able to get back to the vehicle. If they needed everything they could carry on their bodies, they would be facing an incursion of massive proportions. That was something he assumed neither of them would come out of alive, so additional weaponry was pointless. But he wouldn't call in backup. Damian had promised his colleague to do it his way to the best of his ability. He wanted to be safe, so he did his prep, but part of him wished he could make a call to Katie and have her meet him there.

He threw the last bag in the back and closed the door. "Well, that's everything. Now we get some rest in before we head on over there. I'll get the maps ready and addresses down, so we don't get lost anywhere along the way."

As he stepped out from behind the vehicle, he saw Abraham standing there motionless. The man stared into the distance and rubbed his stomach. Damian laughed and, tongue in cheek, asked, "So, how did that pie come out for you?"

The older man scowled. He was still pissed about the whole thing. "I don't think you want to know how the pie came out. What I do have to say is, don't ever eat anything that woman makes. You're a better man than me because that bitch would be ash if I lived here. There would be a pile of dust in the courtyard with her broom lying on top of it. Pretty convenient—simply pick it up and sweep her into the drain before a rainstorm. No proof."

The priest sighed. "We don't do things like that around here. I'm pretty sure that with the way my bosses work, they'd know you had done it before you actually did it. You sure you'll be good to fight tonight? We can wait until tomorrow if you're not up to snuff."

Abraham scoffed and waved his hands before he grabbed a sword from the cabinet. "Please, I'm as nimble and ready as I ever was. Even more so than when I was a young lad fighting next to a young priest in Las Vegas."

He reached toward the blade, and Damian put his hand out hastily. "I wouldn't—"

His warning came too late. The rogue fighter rubbed his finger sideways across the metal to test the blade. Almost as soon as he touched it, he winced and dropped the sword, which clanged loudly on the floor. He hunched over in pain and grabbed his chest and stomach, his face red and his eyes wide. The priest tried hard not to laugh, but he simply had to.

He picked the sword up by the handle and hung it back in the cabinet. Still smiling, he turned and patted Abraham on the back. "I told you everything in this closet is made of special metal. If you even get your hand too close, it will send you into a tizzy. Why don't you head to your room and rest until the pain passes? I'll clean up out here, and when it's time to go, I'll call you. You didn't cut yourself, so it shouldn't take long for you to straighten out. Just remember that tonight when you're fighting. Don't touch the blade, and don't shoot yourself by accident."

"Maybe...I'll shoot...*you*," he growled as saliva dripped from his lip.

Damian chuckled and shook his head. "Go. Lie down. I don't want to have to leave you out here on the floor. And try to relax. It helps soothe the pain a bit."

Abraham turned and hobbled toward the door. Ravi

burst into uncontrollable laughter, unable to hold it back anymore. *Oh, holy hell, that's the funniest thing I've seen in a century. Did he piss himself? I think he fucking pissed himself. That man is the biggest mess I've ever seen. No lie. It serves him right, the way he came rolling into your house with his bullshit.*

Damian tried desperately to contain himself. *You gotta cut him some slack—they stole his wife. But shit, he can't seem to stop kicking himself in the balls.*

The demon laughed even harder. *I wouldn't be surprised if the bitch surrendered herself to them to get the hell out of Dodge. She had to be either as bad as him or woke up feeling like she'd slept with the ugly dude at the bar and regretted it the next day.*

He tried to glare through his laughter. *Aww, she's not like that, although I'm still baffled by the fact that she ran off with him. I don't understand people. He had to be a pain in the ass. At the same time, I've seen some serious change in that man. He's not the same person I used to know, no matter how hard he tries to pretend he is.*

Well, whatever kind of man he was, he needed some serious help in the clothing department. Did you see what he wore when he arrived? He looked like a cross between a hobo and an olden-day Viking. She needs to tame that beast right away.

Damian sighed, his stomach tight from the laughter. *At least he found happiness amidst all the bullshit. I have to say that any Damned would give them both credit for that.*

Ravi wasn't impressed. *I guess. All I know is that we're about to face some serious opponents, and dumbass is over there eating poisoned pie and rubbing special metal. If he wasn't already kicking himself in the dick right now, I would volunteer my services to do it for him. I won't roll in there on my own with him limping in the background. Bro better be on and ready when it's time, or we'll sit our asses right there in the SUV.*

The priest couldn't help but feel the same way, but he wouldn't admit it. He finished repacking the cabinet and locked it, hoping he'd remembered everything. When nothing came to mind, he headed into the house and sat on his bed, then laid back and linked his fingers over his stomach. He stared at the ceiling and tried to create a mental image of success as he imagined the fight in his head. Unfortunately, he still didn't know what to expect. Would there be guns? Would there be mass hand-to-hand combat? Would he be forced to break his vow to the church?

CHAPTER SEVENTEEN

In the driver's seat, Damian looked at Abraham, who stared silently out the window. The man looked calm and collected, and luckily, was no longer in pain. Still, the withdrawn demeanor was unlike him, and it made the priest uneasy. Shrugging it off, he shifted in his seat and looked at the road ahead. They were finally on their way to the school, where they would find out not only Elizabeth's fate but their own as well. Most people would call what they were doing a suicide mission, but he wouldn't let that happen. He had to remember who he was, though, and his companion had to understand that as well.

"I want to talk to you about something," he said into the silence.

The other man cleared his throat and looked at him. "What's up?"

He checked his rearview mirror quickly, and focused on the road ahead as he spoke. "You came to me for help to get your wife back, and I accept that you are the way you are. I need you to do the same for me. I need you to remember that regardless of how you feel about demons, my job is to exorcise as many of the infected in that building as I can. I can't turn that responsibility aside. It was a promise to my church, which makes it a promise to God."

Abraham winced. "Yeah, I don't know about all that."

Damian slowed the SUV. "I'm not fucking playing here. If I stand with you on this, you have to let me do my duty and not simply roll in there and mow down everything in sight. I've respected your beliefs and the way you worked all these years. If you can't even give me that when I'm possibly walking to my death to save you and yours, then I'll let you walk from here."

The older man sighed heavily. "Calm the fuck down, Damian. Have I ever stood in the way of your duties? In fact, I remember many times when I helped collect the bastards to exorcise. I don't like it, that's no secret. I think they should all be killed. Infected or not, they are bad people, and they deserve to get it. I don't understand why you protect them."

The priest put his foot on the brake and drifted to the side of the road. His companion waved his hands in irritation. "All right, all right. Fuck, Mom, don't pull over. You win. I want my wife out safely. I couldn't give two shits about the rest of it—unless someone hurt her. I can promise you, though, that if one attacks me, I won't hold back. I'll blow those bastards' brains all over the wall."

Damian pulled back onto the road, increased speed, and turned his windshield wipers on as it began to rain. It wasn't exactly agreement from Abraham, but he figured it was the best he would get. He was a stubborn man, and in a way, he was right. The humans who were infected in this group were mostly there by choice. The cult wasn't known to turn people against their will. They were white supremacists, hateful people who attacked others based on their background, nationality, sex, or the color of their skin. At the same time, though, Damian knew it wasn't his choice who was saved. Only God could make that choice, whether the people involved understood it or not.

The rogue fighter leaned behind the seat and grabbed the rolled-up blueprint. He spread it out on the dashboard and ran his finger over their point of attack. "I'll go over this one more time. We'll park away from the building, do a little recon, and enter through these doors. As soon as we are in, we look for any sign of these bastards, because we know they will be in there. From there, we'll move through the cafeteria area and the gym. We'll have to improvise if we don't see Elizabeth by this point."

The priest nodded. "Right, but remember, we take care of as many as we can. It won't do Elizabeth any good if you get killed before you can find her."

Abraham rolled the blueprint and smiled. "This should be fun. The whole reason I became a mercenary in the first place was to kill demon scum. Now, I get to kill my second most favorite thing, Nazis. It's like a fucking blue-light special tonight—two for the price of one."

"Let's hope that's the only price we have to pay," Damian mumbled.

He glanced at his companion. The words from his mouth told a big story of courage and excitement, but that wasn't where he was. Beneath the blown-up ego, the priest could see the fear. He was terrified he would lose his wife, and that was what his mind was focused on. Even with the big talk, his eyes would shift to look out the window as he thought about her and what might happen.

Damian knew that everyone had to have one focal point of motivation going into a fight. It was what kept you going when things got rough and really exhausting. This, though? This was different. He didn't have a clear mind going in, something that was almost imperative. He had never seen Abraham like this before, and he worried about his volatility. A rogue fighter not only put their own life in danger, but the lives of everyone around them. Fighters needed to be a team, on point for each other, but they definitely were not that. Abraham was locked onto his own personal wavelength.

The priest didn't reveal his reservations. He simply pressed the gas pedal and sped down the road to finish the three-hour drive. They approached the school along a small road that led to the top of a hill, and he turned his headlights off and parked at the last turn-off. They couldn't risk a heads-up to the demons that they were on their way.

The two men exited the SUV and ducked behind the hedge that lined the edge of the property. Damian glanced at his companion, who had a look of determination on his face. "What do you see?"

Abraham squinted. "I see two at our door but nothing else. They must all be inside at this point."

He nodded, crouched, and headed toward the truck. He opened the back door and grabbed his duffel bag. The rogue fighter stopped beside him. "You ready for this?

Once we're in, it's on. We have no idea what we'll find in there."

The older man readied his gun and shoved it into a holster on his side. "I'll find my wife, that's what I'll find. It's the most important thing to me right now."

Damian pushed his knives into their sheaths and pulled his gloves from his pocket. He slipped them on and drew a deep breath. He was nervous for the first time in a long while, and it occurred to him that he hadn't realized how comfortable he was fighting with Max beside him until the young priest wasn't there.

Abraham put his empty bag in the vehicle. "Can your demon give us any kind of readout? I tried coaxing mine out of hiding last night, but he's not only pissed about being pushed down for so long, he's angry about the pie, too."

The priest chuckled. "And probably also about the metal you touched. Let me talk to her and see what's up."

He grabbed his arm. "You have a she for a demon? I knew it."

"Not now. It's not the time," he retorted with a hard look

The other man smirked and put his hands up. Damian cleared his anxiety. *Ravi, can you do a sweep and see what you can sense?*

She sniffed hard. *Already on it, Pops. Let's see. Huh. Interesting. I would say there are either two dozen lesser demons lurking around in there or a dozen stronger ones, but I can't tell. I can feel the energy and smell their horrid stench, which suggests smaller ones, because those bugs do not understand personal hygiene at all.*

He wrinkled his nose. *Wonderful. Smelly assholes. Exactly what I love to do with my evenings.*

Damian turned back to Abraham. "Either two dozen smaller demons or a dozen larger ones, but she thinks it's more likely to be the first."

The older man looked doubtfully at the building. "And you trust this bitch? I mean, she won't roll us into an army of assholes, will she?"

Ravi growled. *You look here, you piece of shit. I will make it a point that when my body dies, I come back and beat the living fuck out of you.*

He needed her to calm down. *Chill. He's an idiot, so ignore him. I need you focused. I can't have both of you off in some other world.*

She took a deep breath and huffed it out. *Okay. I'm calm, but I'll revisit this later.*

Damian shook his head at his companion. "I trust her, and that's all that should matter to you. Get your shit. Let's get this over with and get Elizabeth back so she can deal with your dumb ass."

He grabbed his bible and patted his pocket to make sure he had his cross. Regardless of Abraham's feelings on the issue, he was determined to exorcise as many of the demons as he could. He shut the door quietly, nodded at the other man, and let him lead the way to the front row of shrubbery. They crouched and stared at the two infected at the entrance. Neither of them appeared to be armed, but the red in their eyes glowed brightly in the early evening dark.

Abraham leaned closer and whispered, "I'll take the one on the right. You go left. Quick, fast, and over with."

The priest grabbed his shirt to hold him back for a moment. "Remember what I'm doing."

He rolled his eyes. "Yeah, yeah. Saving their souls. Whatever. Let's go."

They squatted there for a moment, then jumped simultaneously from cover. Damian used his increased speed to get there first. The older man ground out an expletive, having forgotten that he didn't have any help from his demon. "Damn, I need to get this fool operating again."

The priest leapt and tackled a demon to the ground. He smacked its large paws away and pinned them down with his legs. His hand flew into his pocket to pull out the cross and he held it directly in his target's face. The beast hissed and turned its head. It tried to buck free, but Damian was stronger.

He dropped his bible to the side since he now knew the prayer by heart. "*Ejicio dæmones circa nos, Domine. Civitas nostra expellam eos de populis familiis nos. Tu es salus animarum, Domine. Tuere adiumentique tentationibus nostris repugnantem tenebrarum.* Amen."

The demon hissed wildly and thrashed before rising from the human's chest and hanging momentarily in the air. It disappeared in a vivid flash. Damian reached down and checked the pulse of the host, who was still alive but unconscious. He stood and looked at Abraham with raised eyebrows.

"Hold the fuck still, you piece of scaled shit," the man grunted as he wrestled to hold his demon down.

After a few moments, he gave up out of sheer frustration, grabbed the demon's head, and snapped its neck. Damian sighed heavily and lowered his head as he shook it in open disapproval. The rogue fighter stood, dusted his hands off, and shrugged his shoulders. "Too tough, man. I won't get bitten so you can perform your magic."

While he didn't like this in the least, at the same time, he knew it was the name of the game when fighting alongside Abraham. He would have to come to terms with little assistance from him that night—for exorcisms, at least.

The priest grabbed his bible and stood behind his companion. Abraham steadied himself and glanced over his shoulder. "You ready?"

"Ready as I'll ever be," Damian said as he drew one of his pistols.

The older man kicked the door open and entered, his pistols ready. For the first few seconds, everything was silent before half a dozen demons screeched into the entryway. Damian went left and held his cross up as the beasts sped toward him. He used his arm to knock one of them in the face. As another charged, he leapt into the air and shoved it into the other one's head. They both fell to the floor, and he landed with a boot on each chest.

He thrust the cross at them and started the prayer, but stopped, raised his weapon, and shot a third in the face as it approached with sharp claws extended. He couldn't handle so many of them at one time. "*Ejicio dæmones circa nos, Domine. Civitas nostra expellam eos de populis familiis nos. Tu es salus animarum, Domine. Tuere adiumentique tentationibus nostris repugnantem tenebrarum.* Amen."

His captives barked and screamed as their demons hung on for dear life. The one on the right gave up, and the body went limp as the creature rose out of it. There was nothing Damian could do. The one on the left was still alive, though, and lay unconscious on the floor as its demon spiraled back to hell.

On the other side of the room, Abraham used a round-house kick to knock a demon in the head. It teetered for a moment before it fell to the floor. He yelled, "Here's one for you."

He left the creature there for the priest to take care of and chased after two others who attempted to make a break for it. When he caught up, he grabbed them by the backs of their necks and slammed them face-down on the floor in front of him. He pulled both guns and fired two shots into the backs of their heads. They whined loudly, and Abraham winced. "I forgot about that fucking sound. Like nails on a chalkboard."

The demons turned to ash, and he stepped back to where Damian checked the pulse of the third person exorcised. "Okay, now we head into the cafeteria area. Remember, it's a round room with a pit, so we gotta keep our eyes peeled."

The priest stood, nodded, and clutched both his cross and his gun. "I'm ready. Whatever is in there, we got this."

Abraham smiled with unrestrained excitement. He always reacted that way in a fight. "Time for the pain, motherfuckers."

CHAPTER EIGHTEEN

Damian didn't think twice as he leapt over the half-wall into the pit. He landed on an old table and grabbed the demon in front of him to slam him hard onto the dusty surface. While he held him by the neck with one hand, he shoved the cross into his face with the other, almost touching his skin. The creature whimpered and writhed as it snarled and snapped its sharp teeth.

Damian took a deep breath and began the longer exorcism, because the other prayer didn't seem quite strong enough. "*Domine perpetua Divino Patris, Filii et Spiritus Sancti per unionem cum Divino, quod per Foederatio Immaculati Cordis Mariae, obsecro te perdere the Power of vestri maximum hostium—malis Angelis. Projiceret eos concatenata intima gehennae aeternum Ut possessio tua, quæ tu creatus est regnum tuum, et qui admodum est alicui licentiam. Pater caelestis det nobis divi Augusti temporibus Sacratissimi Cordis Iesu et Immaculatae Cordis Mariae dicatum. Amen.*"

It worked much faster, expelling the demon almost

instantly. The human body collapsed on the table. Damian turned as he heard claws scratch behind him. Another demon was too close. He pulled his gun and fired a bullet into its chest. It tumbled backward, and he stood and fired again, aiming right between the eyes. The beast grabbed its head and stumbled off the table onto the floor. It screamed and kicked and finally turned to dust.

Across the room, Abraham took no prisoners. When he'd emptied his clip, he pulled the swords he had strapped to his back instead of reloading. He jumped up on the half-wall, faced away from the pit, and swept one of the swords through the air. It found contact in the rough-scaled skin of a demon and severed its head cleanly from its shoulders. The body collapsed and turned to ash.

He looked over his shoulder at three adversaries who stood in the pit. With a smirk, he flipped backward off the wall and twisted in the air to land barely a foot away from them. They looked at each other for a second and lunged as one. The rogue fighter dropped to avoid their slashes and ran the sword across their legs. His blow severed the leg from the last one, and the beast lurched and fell to the floor, where it screamed in pain.

The other two grimaced and tried to fight the pain. They teetered, a little woozy. Abraham glanced quickly at the sword, nodded his approval, and sliced the blade across both their necks in one smooth motion. He stomped over to the other demon and stepped carefully over the black goo that had puddled on the floor from the amputated limb. "Looks like you might have missed out on this one, my friend."

With a cold laugh, he raised the sword high and stabbed

it straight down into the creature's face. It pulled out easily, and he felt a rush of excitement as he realized the power of his new weapon. The demon didn't utter a sound, simply burst into ash in front of him. Before he could locate his companion, another adversary jumped from the wall. Abraham swung the blade to shear its head off, and the body slammed into the tables.

He drew his pistol and twirled it on his finger before calmly reloading.

"A little help over here, please," Damian yelled, grabbing his attention.

He looked over his shoulder at the priest, who stood on a table with four demons on the floor in front of him. Abraham chuckled and sauntered toward him. "Put that damn cross away and use a real weapon for once."

One of the demons lunged, and the older man watched as his companion grabbed it by the throat and slammed the cross into its skull. The beast screeched as its skin melted and ran down its face, then its brain bubbled and glopped onto the tabletop below. As it turned to ash Abraham muttered under his breath, shocked by what he'd seen.

Damian shook the blood off his hand and rubbed his forearm across his forehead. "Real enough weapon for you?"

He grinned. "I need to get me one of those, maybe in the shape of the anarchy symbol or something."

The priest simply shook his head as Abraham jumped on the table beside him. "Let's send these bitches back where they belong."

The remaining three demons hurtled forward and raked their long claws through the air. The rogue fighter leaned back, and his boot tipped over the edge of the table. Damian grabbed his shirt collar and pulled him up before he focused on the only infected out of the three attackers. He held his cross before the Damned's shining eyes. *"Domine perpetua Divino Patris..."*

As the creature wailed and fought the inevitable, Damian lowered the person onto the table and drew his gun. He aimed it at the demon that snarled beside him. "You want this one, Abraham? It's not human in the least."

The older man chuckled as he ripped the head off the beast in front of him and threw it over the pit like a football. He pulled a knife from his side and walked toward the other one. "Don't mind if I do."

With a snarl, the demon turned and lunged at him, and the combatants tumbled onto the other table. Damian shook his head as the demon rose from the body of the man he had just exorcised. "Sure, take your sweet-ass time. You're going back to hell in any case."

The creature snarled and gnashed its teeth before it exploded in a ball of light. The screeching stopped. The table where Abraham and the demon wrestled creaked, and the sound seemed to echo off the walls. The priest tilted his head as the adversaries rolled back and forth. The table cracked and the legs collapsed, giving Abraham the advantage. He sliced the knife across the beast's throat and stabbed it in the head.

Breathing heavily, he stood, and Damian jumped down beside him. "You okay, old man?"

He scowled. "Guess I should have taken the time to work out a little more."

The demon below them turned to ash, and the older

man looked around the cafeteria. "That wasn't too bad, right?"

The priest nodded in agreement. "I would say we held our own."

Ravi cleared her throat. *Don't get too cocky. I sense a lot of activity in the gym. Looks like that's their favorite place to be. You know, play a little volleyball, shoot some hoops, sacrifice some humans. The usual.*

He sighed and reloaded his gun. "Ravi says we have a lotta hell on our hands in the gym. Let's get this over with. Elizabeth has to be close."

Abraham clapped his hands. "Rocking, rolling, and fucking stabbing demons. It's my lucky fucking day. Come on, where are you, fuckers?"

Damian raised an eyebrow and watched him bounce over the tables and leap onto the half-wall. The man was like a kid in a candy store. Shrugging at the exuberant display, he hurried over to his companion and they set off along the hallway, alert for any sign of movement. They stopped in front of the gym's tall double doors.

Abraham drew both pistols and smiled. "You ready, priest?"

He gripped his cross tightly. "Ready for some damn scotch."

Ravi agreed. *A-fucking-men.*

They each grabbed a handle and yanked the doors open wide. Their mouths dropped, and they froze. Over two dozen demons with perhaps a dozen infected between them ran across the walls, ceiling, and broken bleachers. There was no sign of an open gate, so Damian assumed they had arrived long before.

In the center of the gym floor, someone had drawn a symbol in what looked like blood. Abraham recognized it as the same symbol he'd seen during the abduction. The six cult members who circled it were all infected humans and all still intact. Lighted candles glowed around them, and a large book lay on a podium in the center. They chanted in a low voice, ignoring the two intruders completely.

The older man wrinkled his nose. "Can you imagine if this was how every basketball game started when you were in high school? First the national anthem and a cult chant, followed by a few incantations to honor the devil before tip-off."

Damian focused intently on the ceremony. "The home team would have an advantage, that's for sure."

"You see Elizabeth anywhere?"

They both scanned the gym, but there were demons everywhere. The priest turned to Ravi for help. *Ravi, do you sense her in here?*

Ravi sniffed. *I sense that she is somewhere in the building, but I can't really pinpoint her location. The scent isn't strong enough to indicate that she's in here. Wherever she is, though...if you don't take care of this, you'll never reach her. They will run you down before you make it to the staircase. Your best choice is to go in with crosses and guns blazing, take out as many as you can, and look for her when you're done. If I can sense her, she is still alive, and at least partly human.*

He breathed, not liking the sound of 'partly' in that sentence. "Ravi said she's here in this building, but it doesn't seem like she's in this room. She said we need to take these guys down first, though, or we'll end up run down by them before we can find Elizabeth."

Abraham gritted his teeth. "What if we're too late?"

He grabbed the man's face and turned it toward him. "That's not the mindset you need right now. Besides, Ravi said if she can sense her, she is still alive and has at least some human in her. That's good news, and better than the worst-case scenario. Let's lock and load, and when we're done, we can find her. I need you to be on the right page, though, or you'll get us both killed."

Abraham pulled his face away and raised both guns in the air. "Oh, I'm in the right frame of mind, all right. The kind that kills fucking demons and doesn't leave a calling card."

With that, he took aim at two demons that crawled across the wall and pulled the trigger. They dropped, and everyone froze in place until they turned to dust. Damian shifted his stance nervously as all eyes turned slowly toward them. "All right then, I guess it's a go. I'll take the infected. You take the demons."

The older man moved forward without a word. The priest rolled his eyes and headed directly for the cult members in the center of the floor. One of them stepped forward and pushed up the sleeves of his robes. Damian put his gun and cross away and prepared for the fight. The infected launched toward him feet-first. The priest waited until the last second and ducked to the side.

As his assailant sailed past him, he slammed his fist into the man's chest and knocked him to the floor. The infected bounced hard, hit his head, and groaned. The priest knelt down and retrieved his cross. "*Domine perpetua Divino Patris, Filii et Spiritus Sancti per unionem cum Divino, quod per Foederatio Immaculati Cordis Mariae, obsecro te perdere the*

Power of vestri maximum hostium—malis Angelis. Projiceret eos concatenata intima gehennae aeternum Ut possessio tua, quæ tu creatus est regnum tuum, et qui admodum est alicui licentiam. Pater caelestis det nobis divi Augusti temporibus Sacratissimi Cordis Iesu et Immaculatae Cordis Mariae dicatum."

The man's eyes widened, and he clutched his chest. "No! Fuck you, priest!"

As the demon struggled to stay inside, Damian punched the victim as hard as he could and knocked him out. With no leverage, the creature emerged and exploded. The priest stood and turned toward the others. He tilted the brim of his hat upward in a mocking gesture. "Who's next? I got plenty of that to go around."

Gunshots rang from the other side of the gym as Abraham raced across the bleachers and fired both weapons toward the ceiling. As he ran, bodies dropped behind him, slammed into the seats, and turned to dust. He pressed on and tried to force his demon to help. "Come on, fucker. If I die, you die too."

Suddenly, his eyes flashed bright red, and he chuckled. "Welcome back. Now, let's kill us some Nazi demons."

He leapt, higher and stronger than before, and grabbed the shot clock hanging on the wall. With his arm around the metal support to hold himself in place, he turned and fired at the floor where a group of demons prepared to attack him. One by one, they fell into a pile before they burst almost simultaneously into dust, which settled lazily onto the floor.

Abraham chuckled to himself, released the magazines from his guns, and inserted replacements. It was a little awkward with one arm still looped around the clock, but he managed. He scanned the room to see where Damian was fighting. One of the cult members had him by the throat. The rogue fighter stuck out his tongue and aimed carefully. He squeezed the trigger and watched as the bullet struck the assailant between the eyes and blew him backward.

The priest put his hands on his knees and breathed heavily. His gaze darted to Abraham hanging from the shot clock, and he nodded. "Wake your demon up?"

The older man gave him a thumbs-up and yelled back, "Hell, yeah, I did. Back to my old self."

Damian mumbled under his breath as he gave him a fake smile. "Oh, great."

They fought their way through the crowd of demons, and he exorcised as many infected as he could. His colleague, of course, didn't discriminate. Anyone who came his way met a bullet to the head. When his magazines were empty, he yanked out the short swords and simply swung at his assailants. Demon bodies fell everywhere, and their residual dust created a smoky haze around them. Screeches resounded throughout the entire building.

Abraham leapt high and flipped over a mass of demons on the floor. When he landed, he spun and slashed his swords through the air. Anything missed by the first sword was decimated by the second. A large beast with long, dangling arms and a snout that extended like a bird's beak charged at him, its teeth shimmering in the candlelight. The rogue fighter sliced at it but missed when he tripped over a body that had not yet turned to dust.

He sprawled on top of it, and the corpse erupted in a cloud of ash. The monster continued its charge. The man braced his hands against the dust-strewn floor and pushed up as hard as he could. He had forgotten his new strength and catapulted into the ceiling. Tiles broke, and he grabbed one of the rafters and shook his head to clear it.

The demon looked up at him and grimaced. With a defiant snarl, it launched itself upward and dangled in front of him by one long arm looped around the same rafter. Abraham swung his body, released his grip, and wrapped his legs around his adversary's waist. He twisted his sword forward and to the side and shoved the sharp tip into the demon's throat. The creature reached up with its large paw and gurgled as its other paw released the girder. They plummeted toward the floor, but the man managed to twist and land on top of it.

On impact, he gripped the handle of the sword tightly and pushed down, using the momentum to sever the head entirely. The demon turned to ash beneath him, and he stood to take in the gym and estimate the destruction and casualties.

From across the room, Damian glimpsed the look of desperation on his face. They needed to find Elizabeth, and they needed to do it now.

CHAPTER NINETEEN

The dozen or so remaining demons dispersed and rushed from the gym into the school. Their claws scratched the floor with a sound much like a million rats scurrying. Damian had managed to exorcise nine of the infected, and the rest of them found their end by bullet or sword. Abraham had destroyed a fuck-ton of demons as he sliced heads off and blasted his guns into them. The gym was covered with dust and ash, and unconscious human bodies lay strewn throughout.

The priest put his cross away and approached Abraham to place his hand on his shoulder. The last of the demons jumped from behind the bleachers and ran out the door and down the hall. They let them go, too tired to give chase. Between them, they had done more than their fair share of killing and exorcising.

Abraham stared around the space, his expression hard and determined. "Now, how do we find Elizabeth? Does your demon still sense her?"

Ravi sniffed. *Still here, but Damian, you have to hurry. Her human scent is diminishing fast.*

The priest forced himself to meet his companion's gaze. "She's still here, but we have to find her. My guess would be upstairs."

The rogue fighter narrowed his eyes and tilted his head, focused on a sudden movement behind the bleachers. He took one step forward and stopped as the last of the cult members from the inner circle stood up. The two men stared at each other for a moment before the infected darted toward the door and headed down the hall.

Abraham put his gun away and hurried after him. "Come on. He'll lead us to her."

Damian sighed and raced after them. He drew his pistol as he ran but had no time to even look around them as they scrambled through the school's hallways. The cultist ahead of them made his way toward the stairs and leapt onto the middle landing. The older man followed and landed as the target climbed the rest of the way up. The priest took the stairs three at a time, using his increased speed from Ravi to catch up with the others. As they reached the top, he put his hand out to slow his companion.

The older man peeked around the corner. "He went into the fourth room on the right. That has to be where Elizabeth is."

Damian understood, but he needed his companion to calm down. "You have to take this in stride. Don't let these few feet be your last because you aren't thinking straight."

They crept down the hall and stood outside the room. A single voice chanted inside. Abraham holstered his gun and breathed deeply. Together, they stepped through the doorway into the room. The priest lifted his gun and shot the cultist they had followed in the head.

Abraham nodded in thanks and looked to the left. Elizabeth lay on a metal lab table and moaned slightly. Her red eyes indicated the presence of a demon inside her. The cult leader leaned over her as he tried desperately to finish the sacrificial spell. "Almighty Invictus, *qota yiz zaeuh, ya aera esaeu called maen qae sabbi grave. Qota sabbi oz o sacrifice. Uza sabbi oq esaeun lizz. Zota sabbi iaiae ya chogabbi yoq la crave, yoq la raph qae fulfill esaeun wishes sabbia aer aony. L'ta iz naoges aes mighty zoedabbi.*"

The rogue fighter snarled and leapt over the desks. He grabbed the man around the waist and dragged him to the floor, but his opponent was stronger than he expected. The cultist kicked him hard in the stomach, and Abraham flew back and crashed into the wall. Without even a slight pause, he pushed upright and shook the dust off his shoulders. His eyes burned brightly.

Damian stood back, ready to go to Elizabeth's side as soon as the leader was incapacitated. Ravi could sense the man's demon. *He has a medium demon in him and won't be easy to defeat.*

The priest grabbed a knife from his belt. *Then I guess I'll have to help.*

He ran forward as Abraham tried to wrestle the man's arms down and stabbed their adversary in the side of the neck. The cultist's eyes grew wide, but he didn't stop. Unbelievably, it was as if the metal barely fazed him. Damian yanked the knife out and grabbed his cross as his colleague held the cultist at arm's length.

He repeated the prayer over and over, determined to

force the demon out. "*Domine perpetua Divino Patris, Filii et Spiritus Sancti per unionem cum Divino, quod per Foederatio Immaculati Cordis Mariae, obsecro te perdere the Power of vestri maximum hostium—malis Angelis. Projiceret eos concatenata intima gehennae aeternum Ut possessio tua, quæ tu creatus est regnum tuum, et qui admodum est alicui licentiam. Pater caelestis det nobis divi Augusti temporibus Sacratissimi Cordis Iesu et Immaculatae Cordis Mariae dicatum.*"

The older man flashed him an inquiring look, but he shook his head. "He's latched on to this human. I can't exorcise him."

Abraham smiled and pulled one of his pistols. "No bother. I'm more than happy to put two bullets in this motherfucker's head. You want to mess with my wife? You want to come into my home and fuck with me? You met the wrong guy."

The cultist laughed. "You stupid sack of meat. You are the one who brought this on your wife. You killed my master's body ten years ago in a battle. Then you pissed on him as he died."

The man thought back and started to chuckle. "Oh… him. That was fun. He didn't really like the golden shower."

His adversary screamed and swiped his hand low to slash Abraham's thigh. The man winced and gritted his teeth before he threw him down and aimed his gun. "Tell your boss that I got more if he wants it, but this time there's a price."

He pulled the trigger twice, and two bullets impacted the man's forehead only seconds apart. The demon emerged immediately, and the body turned slowly to ash on the floor. Abraham spat into the ashes and turned to race to his wife's side. Damian was already there and gave him a moment.

"Hey, baby, I came for you. Hold on, okay? I brought my friend Damian. He'll help you." It was like watching a complete stranger. He had lost his aggression, and his voice had become kind and full of love.

The priest had a knot in the pit of his stomach. He looked at the twisted skin on her body and the way the demon pulsated through her. Abraham looked at him. "Go ahead."

He took a deep breath and began the prayer but couldn't get far. "*Domine perpetua Divino Patris, Filii et Spiritus Sancti per unionem cum Divino—*"

The demon whipped her rigid body from side to side in her husband's arms. Damian swallowed hard and started again. "*Domine perpetua Divino Patris, Filii et Spiritus Sancti per unionem cum Divino, quod per Foederatio Immaculati Cordis Mariae—*"

The monster's claws raked her skin from the inside, and a dribble of blood issued from the corner of her mouth as she gasped and moaned. Her eyes rolled back in her head. The other man held her tightly, yelling, "Don't stop. Save her!"

The priest knew it wouldn't work, but summoned the courage to try one last time. "*Domine perpetua Divino Patris, Filii et Spiritus Sancti per unionem cum Divino—*"

She shrieked, and her body flailed wildly. Abraham looked at Damian with tears in his eyes. "What is happening?"

He shook his head. "The demon inside her is strong. It's decimating her insides with every word of the prayer that I say. He is killing her from the inside out as he tries to hold on. She won't survive this, and there is a good chance her demon will take over before she dies. Trust me, that's not a good thing."

The man sighed and clenched his teeth as he looked down at her still-perfect face. He traced his hand across her cheek and shook his head. Sobbing softly, he leaned down and kissed her soft cheek. "I'm so sorry I couldn't save you, my love. I tried so hard. I promise I will end this. You won't become a demon. You will be at peace."

Damian drew his weapon and stepped forward but his companion shook his head and pushed his hand down. "No, you did your best, Damian. I need to be the one to do this. She needs to die with love, not pity or anger. I need to give her soul the best chance I possibly can. The exorcism won't work. I see that."

"Are you sure?"

Abraham took in a ragged breath and tilted his head back as he wiped the tears from his cheeks. "She is the love of my life. She is my soul and my heart, and I won't let her die by someone else's hand. I won't let this war be the thing that takes her. She is one of the few remaining true warriors."

The priest reached over and squeezed the man's shoulder tightly. "I'm sorry, old friend. We weren't quick enough to save her. To be already so far turned, they had to have Damned her as soon as they took her from your house. I think they did this on purpose as some kind of ritual."

The rogue fighter looked at his wife's face. "They did it as revenge. They wanted to get back at me, to make her what I hate most—a demon. To do this, they stole her life force and snuffed all but an inch of it out and left her for me to take care of. No matter. This is my duty."

Damian reversed his gun and handed it to him. Abraham took it and set it down on the table before he pulled her shaking body close and held her tightly in his arms. His eyes squeezed tightly closed, he rubbed his nose over her ear as he whispered, "My sweet Elizabeth, you gave me more in this life than I ever deserved. You were my soul-catcher, my tamer. Somehow, you held the beast in me down and brought out everything that makes a man human. You were my sweet and strong flower, my everything. With your love, you gave me the world, and I am so sorry I couldn't give you anything of value in return. I failed you, sweetheart. I failed you, and now I have to rectify that."

He tilted his head back and sobbed as he held her close. "Oh, God, if you are out there, forgive me for this. Please forgive me for what I have to do."

Abraham swallowed, leaned forward, and kissed her bloody lips for the last time. For a moment, she went still, the warmth of her body already dissipating. Slowly, he lowered her body onto the table and picked up the gun. As if on auto-pilot, he checked the chamber. He glanced at Damian with tears streaming down his face and pressed the barrel of the gun to her forehead.

He closed his eyes and sat perfectly still. "I love you, Elizabeth. I always have, and I always will. Wherever you end up, I will find you. Wait for me there, in that place we always dreamed of going together."

The sound of the gun going off echoed through the

room. Her body stopped shaking and laid perfectly still. He dropped the gun to the floor, snatched her up once again, and pulled her tightly to him. Light shimmered around her as he held her in the tight circle of his embrace. He closed his eyes, and her body crumbled slowly to ash in his arms. He was left holding nothing but the scarf that had been tied around her neck.

Damian sat in the chair behind him and shook his head as he whispered a fervent prayer.

"God, our Father, Your power brings us to birth, Your providence guides our lives, and by Your command, we return to dust. Lord, those who die still live in Your presence. Their lives change but do not end. I pray in faith for my family, relatives, and friends, and for all the dead known to You alone.

"In company with Christ, Who died and now lives, may they rejoice in Your kingdom, where all our tears are wiped away. Unite us again together in one family, to sing Your praise forever and ever. Amen."

The entirety of everything in both their worlds stopped for those moments, frozen in time. The pain that radiated from Abraham was so strong that even Ravi could feel it from her place deep within the priest. He wanted to help his friend, reach out and make it better, but he knew there was nothing in the world that would remove the pain. They had been too late. They had missed even the slightest chance to save her, but Damian was certain that once that demon had entered her, it was already too late.

Her body had been returned to the earth like all the rest, and he could only pray that someone as pure and good as she was had made her way to heaven. He couldn't believe that his God, the one he served, wouldn't search out and fight for her soul. She didn't deserve that kind of death. None of them did. The innocent were taken, and Damian could feel a renewed desire to save them burning in his chest.

CHAPTER TWENTY

Nearly ten minutes passed before Damian heard a sound from outside the room. The demons who were left were restless. Their leader had been killed, and their future queen eviscerated. They had no one to lead them, but their hunger grew stronger with the smell of the two humans still in the building.

The priest reached over and touched his friend's shoulder. "We have to go. There are demons out there."

His companion lifted his head and looked at him, and his eyes flashed bright red. The priest immediately jumped up to restrain him, but Abraham used the full extent of his demon's powers and was out the door before Damian could stop him. The man was angrier than hell, ready to take out his grief on anything in his path.

He raced after the rogue fighter and watched him snatch any infected or demon who got in his way. The man didn't use his weapons, just his bare hands. His fingers dug into their flesh, and he ripped their bodies apart and threw them against the walls. Black blood splattered the paint-work and lockers, and he left a trail of innards behind him on the floor.

The priest watched as his companion reached up to snatch a demon from the ceiling. He held it in front of him by its throat and stared at it as the creature clawed at his hands and left long scratches down his arms. He felt noth-ing, too pumped with adrenaline and full of his demon rage to care. With an eerie growl, he grabbed his adver-sary's hand, twisted it back, and listened with a satisfied smirk as the bones snapped and popped. The demon shrieked and he released it momentarily, then snatched an arm, ripped it from the socket, and threw it hard into an adjacent room.

The beast squealed and squirmed as black blood squirted from its shoulder. Nothing fazed Abraham at that moment, though. All he could of think of was revenge and he had a burning thirst for the death of every demon in the place. He grabbed the creature's other arm and yanked it off. The sound of flesh tearing sent shivers up Damian's spine. The man snarled and looked into the demon's eyes. All he could see was hate. He just wanted to watch it suffer. The priest stood back in horror and watched as his companion ripped the demon to pieces. Somehow, he kept him alive long enough to feel the pain.

When there was barely anything left, he turned the torso on its side and pulled hard. Intestines splattered on the floor at Abraham's feet. He dropped the two halves and moved on, not even waiting for them to turn to ash. When he reached the top of the stairs, a demon hurtled down another corridor. He raced after it, caught up quickly, and tackled it to the floor.

He held it down with his legs and ripped its arms off to keep the claws away. Relentless, he yanked his knife out and stabbed the beast over and over in the chest and neck. He aimed everywhere he could that wouldn't kill it outright.

Damian walked toward him and saw the blood that ran down the man's face. It wasn't his. Rather, it was dark and evil. He drew his gun, aimed at the demon's head, and pulled the trigger.

Abraham glared at him, and his eyes flashed. "He was mine!"

The priest couldn't allow him to continue the slaughter. He rushed forward and grabbed the man by the shirt collar, lifted him to his feet, and slammed his back against the wall. They stared at each other for several minutes until Abraham froze.

Damian swallowed hard and shook his friend before forcing eye contact. "That's enough! *Enough!* I think you've forgotten how much your wife loved you. You were her savior. You took her out of that world and gave her life. Without you, she would have died as a mercenary long before now. She saw the kindness and sweetness in you that no one else even believed existed. Elizabeth saw the spirit in you that no one else really understood. You aren't this monster. She proved that to you the first time you knew you'd fallen in love with her."

His companion stared intently at him, and his facial expression eased slightly. The priest loosened his grip on his collar and continued, "I know that right now you want something—*anything*—to soothe the pain in your chest. You want anything that will stop the tears and take away the agony and suffering you feel on the inside. But this? It's not the way, Abraham. The display of hellfire you manifested is not the way to do it. You can kill ten demons or a million, and you will never feel the satisfaction or release you're searching for right now."

He looked at the trail of blood and ash. "The demon who started this is safely in the bowels of hell at this moment. Those remaining and the infected work for him, but they didn't make the choice to do this. You want revenge, and I know that feeling. Even as a priest, I know it all too well. Every time one of my brothers or sisters died I wanted revenge, but there is no escape from what you feel except to allow yourself to feel it. You could go down to hell itself and kill the leader, but you would still feel that pit of despair that was just created in your soul."

Abraham tightened his jaw again. "But these motherfuckers are the ones who took her. They dragged her out of her own home, terrified, did ungodly things to her, and put a demon inside her. That monster ripped her body apart from the inside out. He shredded everything perfect about her."

Damian shook his head. "*No!* Her body wasn't what made her perfect. Her guts and her veins weren't what made her the woman you loved. They could never touch that part of her, trust me. They could never take that from her or you. It's eternal and belongs to God. He would never let that be stolen by some demon. You were given the best of her, and she received the best of you. Don't let this turn you. Please don't let this destroy you and bring out the worst in you. She would never have wanted that for you."

A tear trickled down the man's cheek. "They murdered her in the worst way possible."

"I know, brother. I know." The priest exhaled slowly. "This war is far worse than anything we could have imagined. Now, come on. Let's take our stuff and get out of here. There is nothing left for you to destroy."

Abraham's gaze darted up, and he pulled the gun from his colleague's belt. "Almost nothing."

A demon shrieked behind Damian, and he winced as his friend aimed and pulled the trigger to stop the attacker in mid-stride. The rogue fighter looked into his face, his eyes a little lighter. "Okay. Let's gather our shit and get out of here. There's nothing left to do, and there's nothing left for me here."

He released the man's collar and stepped back, reclaimed his gun, and holstered it. The battle had been brutal, and he knew that the other man would never be the same. He nodded toward the room where his wife had been. "Come on. I want to get you something."

The priest walked back into the classroom where Elizabeth had died. His companion stopped at the door and stared emotionlessly at the ashes on the table. Damian looked through the boxes in the room and finally found a beaker with a cork in the top. He removed the stopper and swept Elizabeth's ashes carefully into the bottle with his hand. While he wasn't able to collect everything, he did succeed in gathering most of them. He hated the thought of leaving her remains there in that dank, dark place, although he knew she was no longer there.

He made the sign of the cross and kissed the small crucifix around his neck. As he turned, he could see the deadness in his friend's eyes. He wanted to help him, but he knew there was nothing he or anyone else could do for him. His fear was that the man might be lost for the rest of his life on Earth—a fate almost worse than death for men like him.

Damian handed Abraham the bottle. "Here. That's the best I can do. When we get back, I will find something lovely to put her ashes in. Something you can carry with you."

The older man looked at the bottle, and after a moment's hesitation, hugged it close to his chest. The priest put his arm around Abraham's shoulders and led him out of the room. They traversed the silent hallways past the derelict rooms and down the stairs. The rogue fighter used one arm to steady himself against the wall as he limped across the old floors. A layer of ash and dust coated the entire place.

They both paused at the entrance to the gym and stared inside. The candles had melted into thirteen puddles of wax around the symbol on the floor. A couple of them still had small flames that flickered eerily and struggled to stay alive.

No more demons were left to harass them, and they were able to walk straight through the front doors. Damian patted Abraham on the back as they made their way into the cool night air. They took their time as they walked down the path leading from the school to the SUV. He propped his friend against the vehicle as he took all their weapons, bagged them, and stowed them safely in the back.

The last thing he wanted was to be caught with all that ammunition by someone who didn't understand what they did. His friend's eyes were completely glazed, and he didn't say a word. All the anger had been expelled, and now he faced the backlash of the real emotions. He would have to deal with it, but the priest was sure that at that moment, all he felt was numb. The only real sign of life was that he clung tightly to the ashes, his knuckles white from holding the bottle.

The priest let his gaze drift over the landscape and the sky, which twinkled with stars. It was late—or early, he supposed—but the sun hadn't started to lighten the sky yet. "Come on. I'll take you to one of my favorite pubs so we can get a drink. You could probably use one right about now, and I know I could."

Abraham's gaze shifted to him, and he put on a fake, tight-lipped smile. "Thank you, old friend, but I don't think I'm interested in anything like that. I simply want to get back and take a shower. I don't think they would really want to serve me covered in blood anyway."

He chuckled, but the other man didn't. They climbed into the SUV, and Damian put it in drive and pulled away from the school. His companion leaned back against the seat and stared out the window. Damian watched the lines in the road rush toward him and disappear behind him. His mind went to his past, recalling the faces of all the people he had lost along the way. After fifteen years he was still able to remember every teammate he'd lost, whether they had fought with him for two days or ten years. Their faces were forever ingrained in his mind, and they were the ones who motivated him to continue fighting. They were the ones who kept the guilt away when he had to kill an infected or a demon.

The priest knew the rogue fighter had a huge task on his hands. He had never married, and never would. Still, he had lost many people he deeply cared for. Experience had taught him that the hardest part about all of it was coming to the realization that they were gone and nothing anyone could do would change that. There was no battle, no number of bodies, no hours spent training that would bring them back or ease the pain Abraham would feel in the coming days. Darkness would engulf him, and he would have to be incredibly strong to push through. Those were the defining moments. They were the times you finally realized what you were—or weren't—made of. Were you able to push through to the other side, or would you let the weight of the grief bury you?

Damian could still remember the younger Abraham and what he had been like. He had been reckless and cocky and hated demons with a passion. He did terrible things to them, things the priest had never even thought of. The man wanted to see them suffer and watched the pain in their eyes reflect the pain of the innocent he had seen die horrible deaths. He could understand it to an extent because he had seen children ripped apart, women torn limb from limb, and brave men sent to their graves. Demons didn't simply kill. They *murdered*. They ripped a human's soul from their chest, and they loved every minute of it.

He could only hope that the Abraham who had been

didn't come back to the surface. Deep inside, he wanted so badly for his friend to go back to the home where he'd loved and lived with his wife—and start over. He wanted assurance that he would grieve like everyone else and pick himself up and create a life as beautiful as he could make it without her. Damian knew that was a long shot. He knew that the rogue fighter wasn't the kind of man who would be satisfied with a quiet, lonely life. More than likely he would let the darkness get the best of him, especially since he had allowed his demon to come back to the surface. The two of them were a recipe for disaster.

Even Ravi could tell that from where she was perched. *His demon is low-level, but he is a maniacal sonofabitch. He doesn't care that he's killing his own kind. He simply wants carnage.*

The priest glanced at the man's red eyes. *I know. Abraham has always controlled it somewhat, but now I don't know if he can.*

I don't blame him. I'll be honest, I don't like the guy. I like his style as far as ripping shit apart, but I don't like him. That being said, right now, I feel bad for him. I have never felt a human radiate that kind of pain and hurt.

He gripped the steering wheel tightly. *Let's hope it doesn't turn to something worse.*

CHAPTER TWENTY-ONE

Damian woke early the next day to find the sun shining brightly against the thick curtains in his room. He made a cup of coffee and took it outside, hoping that the morning warmth would extinguish the leftover angst and guilt that simmered in his chest. All night he had tossed and turned, seen Elizabeth's face in his dreams, and heard Abraham's screams as he ran manically through the halls and ripped demons apart. It had been a difficult night, something that felt like a bad dream when he woke up to the birds chirping outside.

He hadn't heard a peep from upstairs, so he assumed his friend was still asleep. He wanted to check on him but decided to give him his space. The man would need it. He was the solitary type, not one who wanted to talk through things. When they had arrived home the night before, Abraham hadn't said a word. Instead, he walked straight inside, grabbed a tall glass, filled it with whiskey, and took it to his room. Damian didn't hear anything else from him for the rest of the night, not that he had expected to. He hoped that whatever he was doing up there would help to settle his heart. This, he knew, would be the greatest struggle he'd ever face.

Even Ravi allowed him to have his moment. Normally, she would have complained to the death about him stealing her liquor, especially the expensive stuff. That night, though, she let it slide. She knew he needed that drink. It showed Damian that there was a little more of a human side to the demon than he had expected in the beginning. It was strange, but he had become accustomed to it with Pandora. Katie's demon had become one of them, and even showed emotions on a regular basis when it came to humans. He'd always chalked that up to her being a fallen angel, but now he started to wonder if there was something more to it.

The priest jostled from his thoughts at the sound of Rose fumbling with her keys. She wore her Sunday best, which included a wild-looking hat with a large flower on top. He'd never fully understood the English and their obsession with hats, but then again, he had never understood fashion at all. Her dress boasted a bright floral print and reached her calves. She wore white stockings and her normal lace-up orthopedic shoes. Her hair was white and curly and waved a little in the breeze. If she hadn't had a demon in her, he could imagine her as one of those old ladies you wanted to hug every time you saw her. Part of him wondered if the demon kept her health up, since she had to be in her seventies but moved like someone half her age.

Rose managed to lock the door and turned. "Oh, good morning. I'm off to church."

Damian smiled and lifted his cup of coffee in greeting. "Very good. And remember what I said the other day. Anytime you need my help, don't hesitate to ask."

She looked away, and after a moment, glanced at him like she was about to do just that. Suddenly, her eyes flashed, and she chuckled nervously. She lowered her head and hurried past him toward the gate. Her gait increased until she walked so fast that he could only assume she was trying to get away before her demon could say anything to him. Still, knowing he'd got through to her human side was good enough for him, at least for now. Eventually, he would have to approach the subject more strongly, but that day would not come soon.

"Well, hello there," a friendly voice said behind him.

He turned to see Max pull his luggage into the courtyard. "Max, you made it back!"

The young man smiled broadly, and his cheerful face helped the thumping in Damian's chest disappear. "Yep, and I did it in one piece too."

He stopped beside the table, stood his bags in a row, and undid the top button of his coat. After a deep breath, he removed his black-rimmed hat and set it on the table. "It's good to be home. I was starting to miss the place."

Damian smiled and kicked out the chair in front of him and the young man sat, still grinning. "I hope you don't mind, but I used some of your coffee. We were out of the old stuff, and I desperately needed something to pick me up this morning. It's been a long few days, to say the least."

Max waved his hands dismissively. "Don't mind at all. I

actually tossed the old stuff because it was gross compared to what I've had recently."

The priest chuckled. "You've turned into a coffee snob. Your demon has created his own little barista monster. I guess it could be worse."

Astaroth scoffed. *Sonofabitch. He drank my coffee, and it smells like the South African brew, too. That's my favorite damn one.* He sniffed and settled a little. *Never mind. It's not worth arguing about now unless I could extract it from his body, which I don't have the energy for.*

In reality, the demon could sense the despair in the air and decided to simply let things be. He had no idea what had happened; he wasn't good at reading things like that. All he knew was that whatever it was, it eclipsed his bitching. Max stared at his mentor for a moment and noted the dark circles under his eyes. Damian never slept much but this was the first time he had seen him look quite so haggard. He was usually up and awake by that point.

Max crossed his legs and furrowed his brow. "I have to admit, you don't seem quite like your normal self right now. You look worn out and tired. What happened while I was gone? You are still in one piece, so I assume you handled it. I don't really know why you wouldn't let me help, but I guess you can explain that to me later."

The priest sighed and put down his cup. "We did handle it. However, it's a long and sad story, and I think I will save it to discuss with you another day. I want to keep things light today." He watched as the recognition of things unsaid moved over his companion's face. "So, how was your trip?"

Max smiled. "It was fantastic. I learned all about the regular history and then the real history of the place. There were so many beautiful things to see there. And the people? Wow, they were so different, and incredibly kind. Apparently, back in the fourteenth century, a great battle took place there. The cliffs were actually carved out by the damaging blows of the demons against the angels. If you look closely, you can still see the burn marks in the stone and rock from the angels' power. All I could think about was Katie fighting some enormous demon there with her golden sword."

Damian raised an eyebrow. "It sounds like you really enjoyed your time there. I'm beginning to think you're more of a nerd than I am. That, my friend, is not okay. I'm not sure I can handle that. I've held the title for a very long time."

The young man laughed and reached over to unzip his carry-on to retrieve a book and a box, which he placed on the table. "I bought a couple of gifts while I was there. I realized when I was looking around that shopping for you is harder than shopping for my mother. I don't know if it's because you have different tastes, or if it's because you are a priest. Most priests, besides the older higher-ups, don't really ask or want anything. I perused the liquor section, but you had everything they offered there. I don't know enough about it to ask for something really special. They looked at me funny, too, because I was a priest. Also, they didn't sell bowties. That was my first thought. I have no idea where you buy those things."

His mentor smirked. "I have had most of them for a very long time, since back when bowties were stylish for everyone, and not only fraternity boys and emo kids. I guess I never let it go."

Max chuckled and handed him a book. "That's about fallen angels. Before I left, I had a bowl of ice cream at the table and flipped through the book you read every night. I guess I was curious as to what you were so enthralled with. Most of the time, you didn't put the thing down, and when you did, I never had a chance to ask about it. My demon said there was a bit of inaccuracy to the information, so I found you one that may be more helpful."

Damian flipped through the old yellowed pages. They contained illustrations, and several pages had hand-written notes in the corners. It looked like a mercenary had at some point, many years before, used the book and made notes about the things they had learned. All in all, it was a very interesting find. He was taken aback by it. "Wow. How in the world did you find this? I can't imagine it being at the local bookstore."

The trainee shrugged. "I took a walk around the city and ended up wandering into an old bookstore down this alley. He had a huge selection of different books, and I guess he catered to a more unique crowd of people like you and me. I asked the owner about a book on that subject, and he retrieved it from a back room. It was covered in dust. I flipped through it and it seemed pretty legit, so I figured you could give it a try."

Damian tapped the cover. "Thank you so much. This is an awesome gift."

Max grabbed the box off the table and handed it to him. "I got this too. Something a little lighter."

He opened the box and pulled out a coffee mug. On the

front was a cross, and on the back, it read, Best Damn Priest Ever!

Max laughed. "I wanted to sharpie in an 'ed' on the end of 'Damn,' but I figured it could work both ways since you are my language monitor here at home."

The priest shook his head at his companion and set the cup down. "You are trying to get me all riled up now, aren't you?"

The younger man put his hands on his hips. "Now I can say 'language' every time you bring that coffee mug out."

Damian pursed his lips. "Probably not your brightest idea. I've thought about having someone re-lay the stone in this entire courtyard. I know a strapping young priest who could use a little lesson in humility, and I think the hard work would do him and his coffee-drinking demon some good. What do you think?"

Max's eyes went big as he scanned the enormity of the space. He put his fingers up to his lips and twisted them like a key turning in a lock. "I guess I will simply smile and be glad that you are enjoying your present. No need for me to throw in extra commentary, right?"

Damian laughed. "My goodness, I think the boy is finally starting to get it. I should send you off on more expeditions like this one. You came back with a little more sense in that thick head of yours. That, or you *really* don't like manual labor."

His companion smirked. "I think it might be a little of both, there."

Just then, the door to the house creaked open, and they both watched as Abraham walked out and squinted into the sun. He held a cup of coffee tightly in his hand and staggered to the table, where he sat heavily in the chair beside Max. Damian smiled kindly at him, and the younger man could tell that something was going on—something he knew nothing about and probably wouldn't for a long time. The man looked rough, even more so than his mentor.

The trainee patted his pants and smiled as he stood and zipped his carry-on. "Well, I guess I should get in there and get unpacked. I probably have some cleaning to do, knowing you. Then there is laundry, and who knows when we will get our next call? I'll see you in a little while."

His mentor nodded. "Thanks for the gifts. They really are nice. You thought about it, and that is what counts."

He nodded and began to walk away. Abraham reached up, grabbed his arm, and stared up at him from beneath the umbrella. Max looked at him with a blank expression. He had been gone for a few days, but he still didn't like the man in the least. At the same time, though, there was something in his eyes—a deep sadness, almost—that struck him in the heart. He didn't know what had happened, but whatever it was must have taken place after he had gone.

The visitor cleared his throat. "No need to run away because I'm out here. I'm not that scary, am I?"

The trainee thought about his answer for a moment. There was something about the look on the man's face that pushed his sarcasm and attitude aside. He didn't feel it would be right to be rude to him, so he shrugged instead. "I gotta put my stuff away. If you're still here later, I'll sit and we can talk if you want to."

Abraham released his arm and breathed deeply in and out. "Nah, I'm good. I've never been very much of a talker anyway, especially not these days. You do your thing, kid, and I'll see you at some point…maybe."

Max looked at him for a moment and smiled before he threw one of the bags over his shoulder. The two men watched as he wheeled his luggage across the paving, careful not to tip it over in the dips and cracks along the way. Damian lifted his cup up to his lips and took a long sip of coffee. He wouldn't approach his companion about anything until he knew he was ready to talk. Instead, he would give him whatever space he needed. It seemed that his attitude was a bit lighter, but he didn't know if there was alcohol in the coffee. Knowing Abraham, it wouldn't be his first drink of the day.

They sat in silence for several minutes, and the priest began to feel like a bad member of the church. It was his job, after all, to help the people, and his own friend sat there in grief and silence. He was about to ask how he was doing, but the man quickly sensed that and cut him off at the pass. "That kid looks like he has a lot of knowledge inside that head. In fact, he kind of reminds me of you, minus the badass fighting. I mean, I don't know if the kid can fight at all, but—"

Damian put his hands up and shook his head. "Don't you dare try to put your wicked ways on my partner. The boy is young, but he's a good kid. I think that's what makes him so good at his job. He has empathy for the infected. It touches him deeply when someone has to be killed or dies from their injuries. He takes it to heart, and it becomes personal to him. That makes him go out of his way to exorcise before he kills."

Abraham rolled his eyes and took a gulp of his coffee.

"That will also be what causes him to lose his life if he keeps responding to things that way. Or he will harden up, because this kind of life has a way of sucking everything out of you and never even says, 'I'm sorry.' Sometimes, I wonder what kind of man I would have turned into if I had never been Damned."

Damian chuckled. "From what I remember you telling me, you were a roughneck before you were infected. I can't see you being very different from what you are today. Not very likable, gruff, grumpy, and generally an unpleasant person."

"Hey, I resent those remarks, thank you very much." He laughed. "No, I actually think you're right. I probably would have ended up in jail or something. Before I was Damned, I came up with a sweet plan to get some money out of the casinos. The demon kind of veered me off track."

The priest sighed. "That's a good thing, Abraham. You say it like you missed out, but I promise it would never have worked. Casinos are like death traps for thieves. They look all shiny, but when you get in there, they watch every single move you make."

His companion looked at him and considered his plan from that perspective. "Meh, you never know. I might have been successful, but you're probably right. I would have ended up in handcuffs and hauled off to a hot little cell somewhere. Instead, I found myself in a completely different type of prison. This one is unbreakable—except by death, of course. It keeps you prisoner in your own mind, in your life, in your actions, and in this crazy shit-storm of a war that we have going on here."

"You're only trapped if you allow yourself to be. I don't

feel trapped. I'm still me. I may have another voice in my head, but I won't let myself slide into the dark. And you should do the same thing."

Abraham said nothing, but the priest knew that was easier said than done for him.

CHAPTER TWENTY-TWO

Damian stretched his arms high in the air and looked out the window at the blue sky. "So, you think you'll hang out here with me for a little while? The weather is supposed to be nice, and it's pretty quiet around here. Except for Rose, of course, but she won't bother you too much since her plan didn't work out."

He set his coffee cup in the sink and turned to look at Abraham, who stood at the kitchen island and ate a handful of grapes, his features drawn and weary. The man scoffed and swallowed. "I don't think I could handle that. You guys are a little too Goody-Two-Shoes for me. I can see us sitting around and contemplating philosophy at the local pub before I finally snap and get into a fight for no other reason than to do something fun."

He laughed. "Come on, we aren't that bad."

His companion lifted an eyebrow. "Yeah, okay. Besides, I've been known to set churches on fire simply by walking across the threshold. I don't want to embarrass you by melting your statue of Jesus. The congregation might hold me down and try to exorcise me or something."

Damian chuckled. "I don't think you're that bad, but I do appreciate the warning. I don't think my boss would be too happy about a melting savior on the pulpit. They might not try to exorcise you as much as drown you in holy water."

"It would boil right over, I'm telling you."

He shrugged. "Maybe it's time we put the church in hot water. It might bring up some revelations I've been curious about for a while."

Abraham popped the last grape in his mouth and yawned. "As much as I would like to help you figure out all the ridiculous past transgressions of your church, I think that might be a little too dangerous for me. A room full of demons? No problem. A room full of clergy? That's what my nightmares are made of."

The priest tilted his head with a mocking smile. "You know, a room full of clergy is also what *my* nightmares are made of. You and I might have more in common than you might imagine. I think my demon would agree with that as well."

Ravi giggled. *As much as I hate to admit anything similar to old less-than-honest Abe over there, he and I are on the same page with this one. I wouldn't wish that torture on anyone.*

The rogue fighter trailed his fingers across the counter. "I've never been good at sticking to one place, at least not before Elizabeth entered the picture. But she's gone now, you know? I don't have any reason to camp out on a permanent vacation, especially not in the house of godly men. That's never been a place I would feel comfortable in. No, I think it's about time I hit the road."

Damian smiled. "Where do you think you'll go?"

Abraham took a deep breath. "I don't really know yet. Me and Liz, we always talked about traveling the world. We had each done it before on our own, but we wanted to do it together without having to worry about busting demon heads. I think I might spend some of my time doing that. I'll go see the world like I wanted to without demon fights in the middle of it all. You know, there are so many things out there that I haven't had the time to really see. This feels like the right time to do it."

The priest liked that idea, although he didn't honestly see Abraham taking in the sights unless it was the local pub. "Do you think you're done fighting demons?"

His companion looked at him with a slight glimmer of red in his eyes. "If Liz were here, I think I could give you a straight answer to that. But with her gone and having died at a demon's hand, I don't think I can say yes to that one. It's too soon, and the pain is too great. I wish I could sit here and tell you that the hunger for revenge isn't there, but it's simmering down deep, and I'm not sure if I'll let it go or do something about it. I have to learn how to live without my wife, and *then* I can figure out what I want out of life."

Damian nodded. "Well, while you're trying to figure it out, don't do things out of emotion. You *will* feel those emotions, that anger and sadness. Don't let it completely envelop you to where you put your life on the line in an attempt to release it."

Abraham smirked, grabbed his bag, and shrugged it

over his shoulder. He walked over and shook Damian's hand. "You know me. I couldn't promise that even if I wasn't wracked with distress and anguish. But thank you, man, for everything you did for me. Thank you for trying to save Liz. I understand that she was too far gone. You might not have been able to save her, but you saved me from simply giving up and letting the demons take me."

"We are family. That's what we do."

He started toward the door but stopped. "Oh, and I promise not to show up and break into your house anytime soon."

The priest fixed him with a serious look. "No matter how much our ideas differ, you know you will always be welcome here. Next time, though, maybe wait outside for me to get home."

Abraham saluted him. "You got it. Next time, I might even give you a phone call beforehand."

Damian pointed his finger at his friend. "Uh oh, you're growing up. I'm so proud of you I could weep. Just be safe out there, or as safe as a man like you allows yourself to be."

When his friend had been gone for about five minutes, he found the house a little too quiet for his liking. Too many events had unfolded in the last few days, and he felt like he needed something to lift his spirits. He walked over to Max's door and knocked.

The trainee yelled from the other side, "Come in."

He cracked the door and gave him a smile. "Come on. I want to take you to the pub for a drink. It's been a wild ride."

Max stared at him for a moment. "And Abraham?"

Damian looked away. "He's gone. He doesn't stay in one place for too long."

The young man grabbed his coat and followed the older priest out of the house. They jumped into the SUV and headed off, ignoring Rose who stood on the corner and glared as they drove past her. She looked slightly disheveled.

The priest reached up and hit the speaker to dial Maps. She answered happily, "Hey, you're still alive. What's up, Pops?"

"Grab your stuff and meet Max and me at the usual pub. We're gonna get a drink and chill out."

She was excited. "I'll be there in ten."

After they found parking, the priest hopped out and waited for Max to situate himself. Maps stood in front of the pub door and greeted them cheerfully. They went inside, grabbed a table at the back, and ordered their drinks. The trainee stuck with a soda this time, Maps ordered a Gin and Sprite, and Damian asked for his normal scotch.

Maps leaned forward. "Tell me about Abraham. How in the world did you guys get to be so close?"

He smiled. "Well, we met not long after I became a merc. He's an outsider, a rogue fighter who works alone. Sometimes, I liked to break away and fight demons on my own terms. Anyway, there was this one fight... It was Abraham and me, two guns, and two rounds of ammo. We stood there and faced off against two giant demons. Those things were gnarly, at least twelve feet tall, with fists like hammers. We were already neck-deep, so we figured we were in it for the long haul. In the end, he saved my life. I was about to be a smashed priest in an old broken-down warehouse where no one would have ever found the body. I would probably have turned to ash, though, come to think about it. After that, we always had each other's backs despite our differences of opinion about life and religion."

She shook her head. "He was so brash and out there, like he gave zero fucks about anything. It made me crazy."

Max laughed. "He kind of reminded me of you in that way—rough around the edges, and said whatever came to his mind. Of course, you show that you're a good person. Him? Not so much. He was more like Stalin on the outside with a dash of teddy bear hidden somewhere in his liver."

She shook her head, laughed, and stood to ruffle his hair. "Gonna make my rounds."

They watched her as she flitted around the bar and greeted her clients. Damian studied Max, who looked a lot more content than he had before he'd left a few days earlier. "You look less stressed. Before you left, I thought you would have a breakdown. I didn't want to send you, but it looks like it might have been for the best. Are you feeling better about everything?"

Max stretched his arms languidly. "You know, after that trip, I do. I learned so much about history and the demons and how much they have affected us. I learned about all the people who have died before us, and how many people are affected by all of this. It gave me a wider perspective. Not that I like to see anyone die, but I can see the whole picture now, not only the issue right in front of my face. Nothing will alter the fact that any life lost is terrible, but opening my mind up helped a lot."

Damian lifted his glass and clinked his companion's. "Good. I know this is all a hard transition, but you're good at what you do because you care. I want to make sure you never lose that."

"Like Abraham?"

He smirked. "I don't know if that man *ever* cared, much less lost it."

Max looked quickly from side to side and leaned in. "So, I was thinking. If my goal is to disarm an infected, then I need to get better at hand-to-hand stuff. I wondered if you would work with me more on offensive and defensive karate moves?"

The priest was enthusiastic. "Hell, yeah. The more prepared you are, the better you'll be. Your demon can help you, too."

The young man looked curiously at him. "I wondered why Abraham was still limping. Shouldn't his demon have taken care of that by now?"

Damian shrugged. "He suppressed his demon when he married his wife because he wanted a real life. Now, the demon came back out and helped during a fight, but I think they have to reestablish a relationship before he helps Abraham with much beyond not dying. Everything he has done for years has been with his natural human strength and willpower."

Max was shocked. "Really? Wow. I have to admit I have a little more respect for him now that I know. I can remember the struggle of being all human, and I don't know how I'd do it without Astaroth. I wouldn't be very good at fighting demons, for one thing, and he has even helped me conquer some fears. I guess Abraham is a lot stronger than I thought."

"Yeah. I only hope he keeps that in the coming days."

Before the trainee could ask what he meant by that, Maps returned to the table. "So, Maximus, I heard you took a little trip to Blanch Land. Got out of London for a little vacation. I bet you met all the girls and left broken hearts in a trail behind you as your plane took off."

He merely looked at her and blinked. "I couldn't have done that, even if I wasn't a man of the cloth. Believe it or not, when I take the uniform off, I'm still the same person."

Max laughed as she feigned shock.

She leaned on her hand. "So, what did you do while you were there?"

He was excited to talk about it. "Well, I started by touring the town and learning about its history. The place is actually really interesting. It was built in the early 1600s by a bishop, but what people don't know is that the man had a demon inside him. He made it look like he was creating a sanctuary for the people, but he really wanted the power that went with it."

Max paused, and his mouth dropped as he stared at her. She had closed her eyes and was making really loud snoring sounds. Meanwhile, his mentor whispered to the waitress and sent her off with an extra tip. The young man knocked Maps' arm out from under her, and they all laughed. When the waitress returned to the table, she delivered three shots of whiskey and set one in front of each of them.

Damian raised his shot glass. "To surviving another round of demon infestation."

His companions held up their shots. "Hear, hear."

They drank, and Maps laughed at Max when he choked a little on his. They sat talking and laughing for a couple of hours until Damian noticed the trainee had started to fade. "Hey, Max, why don't you go on outside and get some air, and we'll head home? I'll be right behind you."

The young man nodded and blinked his eyes. His companions chuckled as they watched him skip out the door. Damian shook his head and turned to Maps. "Here's the money for the books and the work. You were a lifesaver, I won't lie. Everything I get done is because you're there feeding me information."

She smiled and pulled a book from her bag. "Here's another one. Enjoy. I'll hang out here for a bit longer. I don't feel like heading all the way home."

He gave her a hug. "Be careful."

Her thumbs-up matched her cheerful smile, and he headed for the door, his new book clutched to his chest. He was stoked to have so much reading material about fallen angels, with the book Max had given him and now another from Maps. There was no way he wouldn't figure something out from all of it. It would be a good night by the fire.

CHAPTER TWENTY-THREE

Later that night, when Max had passed out in his bed, Damian wandered into the living room and plopped down in the chair. He pushed the poker into the newly-made fire and leaned back as he drew in the warmth and comfort of it. His mind moved immediately to Abraham and everything he had gone through. Elizabeth had been a good merc, and from what he knew about her, she had been a really wonderful person as well. She really cared about people, which was why she had signed up to fight even though she wasn't infected.

His thoughts about the rogue fighter had always been ambivalent. He had known the man for almost fifteen years and fought beside him, which meant he knew almost everything there was to know about him. Thinking back, he couldn't say that he had been a trustworthy guy or even really that good a friend to him. However, in the present situation, he felt incredibly bad for him. In his mind, it would be no different than if Korbin had lost Stephanie or vice versa. They were connected in a way that Damian didn't fully understand.

Ravi sighed. *The last time I came to Earth, I felt my real first emotion.*

He was surprised. *Really? What happened?*

The tone of her voice was different. There was a whisper of sadness in it. *I made a friend. She was my first friend, and we did everything together. I knew the world was a dangerous place, so I did whatever I could to protect her. This was during the forties. We went out to a club to dance, she met some guy, and he dragged her off. In the end, he and his buddies killed her. The worst part about it was that they were demons. My own kind killed my best friend.*

Damian's heart went out to her. *Ravi, I'm so sorry about that. It doesn't matter whether you've felt emotions your whole life or only for a moment. Losing someone is difficult.*

She sighed and brightened. *Yeah, well, that's the thing with you meatsacks. You break so easily. You're like a bunch of porcelain dolls walking around the planet. One strong storm and you snap like a twig.*

He chuckled. *I'm surprised that you made a human connection like that.*

Well, you have to remember something, old chap. A lot of us were once creatures of God too.

The priest tilted his head to the side, shocked by that statement. He had always assumed she was a regular demon like all the others he had come across—besides Pandora, of course. It made him think that she knew more about fallen angels than she was willing to admit. Before he could bring up the subject, though, his phone vibrated in his front pocket.

He pulled it out and smiled, seeing Katie's name on the screen. "Well, well, if it isn't the prodigal daughter. It's good to see your name pop up on my phone."

She laughed. "And it's good to hear your voice. Timothy told me you called a couple of days ago. I've just been insanely busy."

Damian grinned. "That seems to be the way with you. I don't remember you ever *not* being busy in some way or another. What is it this time? Satan himself?"

Katie scoffed. "Yeah, right, I wish. Then I might be able to end this war. No, there was a possible Leviathan sighting. The beast goes around bustin' up cities and then slinks back into the water. Then there is my condo, which we moved into. There are a few things that I still want to get done on it. We also had the whole 'getting Korbin and Stephanie settled in with their memories' and such, and Calvin's and his girlfriend's drama. There seems to be so much happening that I can barely keep it all straight. Luckily, they were here when the base was attacked, but Stephanie got pretty beat up."

Damian nodded. "That's right. You're making the move soon."

She groaned. "Yeah, we hope. It's all up in the air right now. I'm trying to keep it together."

"I do wish I was there. I heard the whisper about the attack on the base. I'm sorry you lost men out there."

As he talked, the sky opened, and rain began to pour down outside. Thunder rolled through the clouds, echoing through the house. He liked it, and always had. Storms seemed to soothe his soul. On top of that, he had the opportunity to talk to Katie, which was always a plus for him. He leaned back in the chair and put his feet up on the ottoman, finally feeling his shoulders begin to relax.

Katie told him all about the fight at the base. "It was insane. I got there in the nick of time. Anyway, what have you been up to? Any good fights?"

Damian snorted. "Actually, yeah. I had an old friend show up out of nowhere a few days ago. His wife was taken by a cult, and we had to track her down to this school and fight our way in. There were dozens of demons all over the place. I was able to save quite a few of the infected."

She sounded worried. "What about the woman?"

His heart sank a little. "Sadly, we were too late. In fact, even if we had gotten there right after they abducted her, we would have been too late. It was a huge fight. It's probably the biggest I've been in without a whole team with me."

"Good Lord, Damian, you should have called me. I would have come and helped you fight those bastards. Three is a lot better than only two."

He smirked. "Yeah, but you have your own issues to deal with there in the city. Besides, it's my job to do this. I know when to ask for back-up if I need it."

Katie laughed. "Oh, yeah, you *definitely* know your job. You trained me, after all. Last night, I went to a nightclub in the city to bust up some demon rings. I got them all on the run, except one bolted out of the club and hightailed it right out of the reach of the police. I swear the cops here aren't the brightest crayons in the box when it comes to stuff like that, but when they lost that demon, they were pissed. The other precinct will never let them live it down."

The priest shook his head. "I think it's too dangerous to

put the cops on these things, but I guess someone's got to do it. Are you working with them or training them?"

"Training them. They need to be able to handle the small-time infected, so I don't get called out for a loud house party or something."

Damian rolled his shoulders and felt the tension release. "How's the team doing?"

"Oh, super well. They keep up with everything, and try to make life easier for me." She laughed.

He was glad to hear that, at least. "Well, I miss you guys, that's for sure."

Katie paused for a moment. "Damn. Hey, I'll give you a call soon, okay? I have a call coming in from the general, and he gets impatient."

The priest nodded. "Got it. Stay safe out there."

"You too!" she yelled back.

He hung up and smiled to himself as he placed his phone on the table. Ravi was ready to talk as soon as he hung up, which made him think she was diverting the questions on fallen angels she knew he wanted to ask. *So, when will you take me out shopping? We talked about it before, and you said you would think about it. I mean, at least take me to a couple of places. I'm dying to see what the new fashions are, even if they're only men's fashions. I promise to keep your style, but perhaps update you a little bit.*

Damian picked up his glass, took a swig of whiskey, and rolled his eyes. *Why not? I guess I should get with the times.*

She cheered. *Oh, this is fucking awesome.*

But, he interrupted, *I'm not getting rid of the bowties.*

He looked up as Max stumbled through his bedroom door, his hair sticking up everywhere. His eyes were almost completely closed, and he didn't even look at his mentor. He wandered into the kitchen and opened the cabinet door. Damian leaned forward to watch him and make sure he didn't hurt himself.

He poured a glass of water and guzzled it down, and droplets rolled down his chin. When he was done, he put the glass on the counter and shuffled back into his room. He shut the door without a word, and the priest frowned. The kid was strange. Max did that at least three times a night, and he wondered every time if he was actually awake or if he was sleepwalking. He always tried to remember to ask him about it but figured it wasn't a big deal. It wasn't like he pissed in the fridge or took the SUV for a joyride with a flower pot on his head. He was merely staying hydrated.

Damian jumped as he heard him slam into some piece of furniture. The young man's voice echoed from his room. "Sonofabitch!"

He jumped from his chair and hurried across the room to throw the door open. He looked at Max with concern and at the nightstand on the floor. However, instead of asking him if he was okay, he simply looked at him and smiled. "Language!"

Before his companion could respond, he slammed the door. Damian laughed as he resumed his seat. He loved giving the kid a hard time, especially when he didn't expect it. It had started to become his favorite thing to do, and he felt better that things were back to normal in the house.

Damian grabbed the book Max had given him and opened it to the first page. *This book is a comprehensive over-view of the history of fallen angels. All accounts in this book came from clergy members, mercenaries, and those who work closest to the demons on Earth. Accounts can be traced back to prior historical teachings, and are certified to be true to the best of our knowledge.*

He scanned to the end of the page, where there was a short handwritten note. *Try certified by complete morons.*

The priest laughed loudly and shook his head. "At least if there is commentary, it's humorous."

He flipped through the first page and read the text and the notes on the side. Some of them were only names and other snide comments about the angel being discussed. One of the comments made him stop and focus for a second. *Gabriel, the angel at God's hand. More like the angel that makes me fucking miserable every time I come to Earth. He needs a good dick kick.*

Damian lifted an eyebrow when he realized that whoever made the notes was a demon. Not only that, they had a surprisingly similar sarcastic personality to none other than Pandora. It couldn't have been her, though, right? The thought seemed crazy, and he laughed at himself and decided that he missed everyone more than he'd thought.

He turned the page and continued reading. The thunder rumbled loudly through the whole house and shook the pictures on the wall. He closed the book and leaned forward, a chill running down his spine. Right then, someone pounded hard on the door, and Damian wondered who needed to visit that late at night.

There was only one way to find out…

THANK YOU for not only reading this story but these *Author Notes* as well :).

(I've always been good with opening with thank you… If it's not good, I need to edit the other *Author Notes*!)

RANDOM (*sometimes*) THOUGHTS?

I started writing (and releasing) stories in November of 2015. In just a bit over a week, it will be the third anniversary of my first book, *Death Becomes Her*.

(See on Amazon.com here: My Book)

Since I first published, I've been blessed beyond what's normal in the publishing arena. From meeting fans around the world to supporting and releasing collaborations with super-talented authors (who often write better than I do) to starting one of the largest Indie Marketing-focused Facebook groups (20Booksto50k®) presently active.

I'm constantly astonished by how this company has grown, and I don't totally understand it. I hope we continue to produce stories (maybe not all of them, but more than enough) that entertain you and make you pump your fist in the air or wake up your significant other laughing in bed late at night.

If you are reading this from a hospital bed or your own bed and aren't feeling well, I hope we alleviated some of your pain for a while.

We love you!

HOW TO MARKET FOR BOOKS YOU LOVE

We are able to support our efforts by you reading our books, and we appreciate you doing the below!

If you enjoyed this or ANY book by any author, especially Indie-published, we always appreciate it if you take the time to review a book, because it lets other readers who might be on the fence to take a chance on it as well.

AROUND THE WORLD IN 80 DAYS

One of the interesting (at least for me) aspects of my life is the ability to work from anywhere and at any time. In the future, I hope to re-read my own *Author Notes* and remember my life as diary entries.

So (*for future Mike*) I am sitting at the end of the bar in the pizza restaurant "FIVE 50" inside the Aria Hotel Las Vegas. You are sitting at the end of the bar in the back (from the front door.)

FAN PRICING

If you would like to find out what LMBPN is doing, and the books we are publishing, just sign up at http://lmbpn.com/email/ . When you sign up, we notify you of books coming out during the week, any new posts of interest in the books and pop culture arena, and the fan pricing on Saturday.

Ad Aeternitatem,

Michael Anderle

Hi there!

First, thanks for picking up a copy of our book 2. It's been a wild ride with Damian. Hope you're enjoying the new series. We are.

It's getting cold up here in Maine, which I'm not at all used to. We were at lunch yesterday with our HEAVY coats on in the restaurant, and the waitress asked, "You guys cold?"

I wanted to say, "Here's your sign." But I'm a sweet girl, so I just smiled and nodded.

She laughed. "It's only 40 degrees outside. It feels great."

"We're from Texas." I lifted an eyebrow and shivered.

More laughter. Now she gets it. 40 is the dead of winter for us! It's *cold*.

Hopefully, you're snuggled up by a fire this coming weekend, catching up on a great adventure between the pages of a book. I know that's where I'll be.

As always, Mike and I appreciate you so much for taking this journey with us. It means the world to us.

Slave to Many Stories,
Laurie Starkey

CONNECT WITH MICHAEL TODD

Want more?

Find us On Facebook

https://www.facebook.com/Protected-by-the-Damned-193345908061855/